Pastor Dale

IN THE MOMENT

With Regards
S. Brength

IN THE MOMENT

Short Stories

Sandra M. Bringer

iUniverse, Inc.
Bloomington

In the Moment
Short Stories

Copyright © 2012 by Sandra M. Bringer

All rights reserved. No part of this book may be used or reproduced by any means, graphic, electronic, or mechanical, including photocopying, recording, taping or by any information storage retrieval system without the written permission of the publisher except in the case of brief quotations embodied in critical articles and reviews.

This is a work of fiction. All of the characters, names, incidents, organizations, and dialogue in this novel are either the products of the author's imagination or are used fictitiously.

iUniverse books may be ordered through booksellers or by contacting:

iUniverse
1663 Liberty Drive
Bloomington, IN 47403
www.iuniverse.com
1-800-Authors (1-800-288-4677)

Because of the dynamic nature of the Internet, any web addresses or links contained in this book may have changed since publication and may no longer be valid. The views expressed in this work are solely those of the author and do not necessarily reflect the views of the publisher, and the publisher hereby disclaims any responsibility for them.

Any people depicted in stock imagery provided by Thinkstock are models, and such images are being used for illustrative purposes only.

Certain stock imagery © Thinkstock.

ISBN: 978-1-4620-8390-9 (sc)
ISBN: 978-1-4620-8392-3 (hc)
ISBN: 978-1-4620-8391-6 (e)

Printed in the United States of America

iUniverse rev. date: 01/20/2012

To my children, their children, friends, and all those who refrained from laughing out loud at my attempts to write, I thank you. Thanks also to any and all readers who enjoyed at least one story, had an affinity for a particular character, or simply bought my book on a whim and were only mildly disappointed. I will keep trying. I have more stories to tell.

Contents

Introduction ix
The Women of the Family 1
American Blue Eyes 9
Back Issue 18
A Spinning Top. 21
Rapture 31
Her Ex. 33
The Wedding 37
The Funeral 42
Bozo Hair 51
Anna. 54
Johnny 59
Forgiven 62
The Halloween Bash 70
Dave, the Bus Driver 77
    Maudy. 81
    Tanessa 85
    Will Sees Rebecca for the First Time 87
    Dave and the Harvey Twins. 91
    Cowboy and Rebecca 96
    The Killing 102
    Rebecca. 108
    Epilogue 113

Introduction

Does an event define a life, or does the individual define the event? Is it a combination of both, or is it another equation entirely? It's a philosophical question that begs an answer, but as we observe individuals in our own lives, on the news, or in other ways, many of the actors in an event appear not to have the insight, ability, time, or chance to reflect on such matters. The moment is now, good or bad. It is right now. Questions go unanswered, and not all the information is there. Still, a moment in a person's life can say volumes about his or her character. We may never know more than we do now; the next step in life's dance is conjecture, a mystery, an uncertainty—but its part in the story is vital nonetheless.

May this collection of stories and reflections on ordinary individuals caught in the moment challenge you to ask questions that loom about the people in your life. Perhaps these stories will prepare you for, or help explain, the moment or event that defines you.

The Women of the Family

Big Bull is as large as his name implies, and all of him is sitting uncomfortably on his heels, his arms tightly at his side. He is trying to hold his body in, while Stinker is furiously swaying side to side, side to side. Bull must maintain his awkward position. Quietly and carefully, he waits, trying not to let his belly touch Stinker. Slowly and softly like a rising balloon, Bull lifts himself upright on his knees and raises his heavy, muscular arms up to shoulder length, holding stiffly, straight out, turning his Lava-scrubbed hands palm-side up, thus shortening the span of Stinker's sway. In this way, Bull manages to form a safe haven with boundaries for Stinker. The boy can still move, but not as hard and fast as before.

Bull is breathing fast, as if he is moving side to side too. With Stinker at a tolerable pace, Bull stops gulping for air, and his big chest slows and moves with the tempo set by Stinker.

"Rest, boy. Please be still!" Bull repeats over and over. It's as if Stinker has an inner metronome; no one knows what tempo he's in, or who or what sets the boy's tempo. Bull has stopped himself from shaking the boy or holding Stinker down to still him more times than he can count. Stinker is not the child's given name; he is dubbed Stinker because of his toilet accidents. The name just stuck. Bull would stay on his knees the rest of his days if it would fix Stinker.

Bull's half-sister dropped Stinker off about a year ago; she could not care for Stinker. Her son, barely potty trained, unable to speak properly at four, with agitated and swaying fits that lasted hours, was unbearable to her. "What does the boy want?" Pale to semitransparent, small for his age, the boy was failing to thrive; Bull's family had to take Stinker. A telephone call asking how Stinker is doing is all Bull and the women of the family expect from her now.

Stinker is better off at Bull's home. He eats for the most part, or allows others to feed him. He points to things he wants, there are enough people in the house to check for him when he goes missing, and everyone is used to him. But Stinker is backtracking of late. His bouts of swaying have increased. Fluttering his eyes at the ceiling, still moving side to side, the boy has not eaten or drunk since yesterday.

"What sets you off, boy?" Bull says. "You got to eat, little man!" Bull must stand before his legs go dead. He lumbers to his feet and gently pats the air near Stinker's head.

An auto mechanic by trade, with his own shop and a couple of workers, Bull knows his job. He is good at it, and he has had the sense to speak to doctors about Stinker. Recommendations from experts like "institutionalize" sound a lot like "incarcerate" to Bull.

"Words that grown men can hardly spell can't be right for a tiny boy," is Bull's reply to the experts. "You don't put your family out. The boy's not an animal to be cut from the herd!" Bull might not be able to mend Stinker, but he is confident that the women of the family can bring the boy around; they will not let the boy perish.

"Little man, Uncle Bull's got to run. Godmother is scooting across the lawn right now, and the house is going to be jumping with ladies in a minute. You hide yourself, and someone will come fetch you when the party's over. Go slow now. Go slow." He said it with his usual hope. Bull would will Stinker to be at peace if he could.

Godmother, the self-appointed head honcho of the clan, dressed in purple polyester pull-on pants with a matching sequined sweatshirt, is heading toward the house with great determination. She bellyached to the entire family that a combined wedding/baby shower is "Totally out of line! Booties and toasters, I can't believe it!" When no one paid her any mind and went ahead with the double-duty shower for Maxi, Godmother had no choice but to attend the combination shower and put herself in charge of the event.

Meanwhile, in anticipation of Godmother's management, Maxi and Becky, Bull's daughters, and his wife, Martha, are busy readying the refreshments and decorations for the event. Mary, one of Bull's sisters, lives in the large old farm home as well, and since she and several friends of Maxi are the official shower givers, the family home is simply the most convenient location, with the most space.

Barbara, a favorite niece of Bull, has three children and is to be the maid of honor. She is a real "work" according to Godmother, flashy and not one to take any lip. Barbara expects confrontations with Godmother, though admittedly, she admires the "old bat."

Ally, Martha's daughter from her first marriage, and her two children are also part of the wedding party. She is comfortable with Stepdad Bull, and she loves Maxi and little Becky. She is happy to be included in Bull's extended family of mostly women.

It takes an atlas to differentiate between and count the women in Bull's family, and they are often a part of town talk. Begrudgingly, the talkers give them their due, however. They take care of their own, it is agreed. Stinker is proof positive of the family fidelity. Cleverly, the talkers are most often included in family events and parties. It helps to moderate the gossip.

Girlfriends from high school are milling about the kitchen with Max. Another woman, a distant cousin, appears out of nowhere and helps to open chip bags and put dip in little glass dishes. Ally and her brood are crepe-paper twisting. The balloon-blowing task is delegated to whoever passes by with wind in them. Bull appreciates and knows by name each woman invited, a lone rooster in a full hen house. Courtly in his way, Bull never struts or crows his position.

Godmother, put out by the fact that so many hands are on board with the preparations, marches into the kitchen. She orders this woman and that, dictating the best way to arrange the sandwiches on the trays, the proper way to decorate the Jell-O molds, and when to play the party games. She gives opinions to all within earshot. "The orange sherbet for the punch must be added when the last guest arrives," she warns. It is a marvel that each woman continues doing exactly what she is doing, yet obeys each of Godmother's orders to the letter.

"Where's our Stinker?" Godmother looks around suddenly. "Did he eat this morning?" she demands to know.

"I'll check on Stinker. I saw him with Bull," Mary whispers to Martha.

"I tried to force milk on him about an hour ago," Martha says quietly. "Our girls are so noisy and strong willed, and God bless us, no one can say we don't eat!" She laughs while patting her midriff. "I just don't know how to help the boy sometimes."

More guests begin calling hellos at the back and front doors all at once. Older women are dressed in Sunday best, and Maxi's peers are in jeans and tees with junk bangles or short sundresses. Godmother runs to direct traffic.

Gifts fill the table near the decorated chair Maxi is to sit in, and the living room and front porch area fills with laughter and chatter. Windows are open, and the curtains move with the commotion. Whiffs of different lotions, colognes, and sprays roll off the women as they move this, pick up that, and admire the crepe-paper streamers and white balloons taped on the mantelpiece. Maxi, kissed and kissed, smiles at the attention received from everyone.

Godmother, in her militant fashion, begins filling punch cups, elders served first, gulping her cup. She supervises the children's plates and piles a big plate for Maxi. Bull comes in, waves a quick hi, grabs some food for the men who remain on the stoop with him, and runs out. Godmother, a wonder, continues running the show and giving orders while spinning trays in front of the guests.

In the Moment

A happy crew of young women escort Maxi to her seat of honor. With the current tattoos of fashion on her ankles and one arm, and her many ear piercings, Maxi looks splendid to her peers. The mask of pregnancy and the darkening around her eyes gives her an exotic, almost regal look.

Godmother interprets her beauty as possible nausea and immediately worries aloud that "Maxi might be one of those crazy women who don't eat for fear of being too fat!" She further speaks these and other assumptions to Maxi's mother. Now Martha can worry with her.

Maxi notices mother's and Godmother's focus on her belly. She tries to will herself to feel less queasy, but she cannot look at the huge plate of food Godmother put next to her. "She's a mind reader, Godmother, that's what she is!" she mutters under her breath.

"Some law and order, please!" Godmother shouts, quieting and forcing any women roaming free to sit. "The designing-of-a-wedding-dress-by-using-toilet-paper game will commence," Godmother announces. Gleeful teams form with all manner of bustle and laughter. Godmother, of course, refuses to participate in such foolishness. Barbara surrounds her with several like-minded women, and they in a flash wrap her up like a mummy. Her bite never matches her bark, and she submits as the din escalates.

Predictably, the flower girls, including Becky, plus Great-Grandmamma on the groom's side, with her highly toilet-paper-decorated walker, win the prizes. Aunt Mary de-mummifies Godmother and brushes her cheek with a kiss as Barbara hands out the prizes.

Free of the toilet-paper wrappings, without missing a beat, Godmother springs forward and announces the guessing-of-how-many-colored-coated-wedding-almonds-in-the-jar game, with a baby-name game to follow, plus a contest about the favorite groom's likes and dislikes. "The woman's a hoot 'n' a half," someone says.

With the games finished, "It is time to open gifts!" Godmother bellows. "Let the oooing and aaawing begin!" Future thank-you notes require the recording of what is in each package and from whom, which Godmother starts, but Mary finishes the chore. Barbara and Godmother are too occupied with loud and prolonged ooos and aaaws to continue.

With the gifts opened, in order to prevent Godmother from proposing something else to do, music is switched on, and the younger women and Maxi dance to the blare. Remaining sandwiches pass around, and Maxi and all are called to eat the "all-purpose-shower cake" by Martha. Infants are getting cranky, toddlers are restless and need help with their cake, and little Becky tells Maxi she is taking cake to Stinker. Godmother gives the nine-year-old a generous pat on the head.

Three hours of partying flies, women and children mill and stream to and from the living room to the backyard, and other places in the house, men and cars are arriving. It is time to go, and on cue almost, the women, in a whirl of activity, begin packing up, gathering children, kissing good-bye, and heading out the door.

Godmother and Barbara run after the leaving guests, making sure each has a party favor, and they remain together at the door until the last guest departs, though each gives the other a wary look.

"That was work!" Godmother exclaims as she melts into a comfortable chair, with a pat on her hand from Martha. Mary, the only woman in the family Godmother never gives orders or raises her voice to, stops folding chairs and rushes to retrieve Stinker. The party roar has softened and waned; he will be able to sit among them. The few party stragglers left are close family. Actual periods of quiet hang in the house, and as Maxi inspects her gifts and makes comments, they all nod in perfect agreement. The mechanics of straightening up are restful.

Stinker is behind the pantry door, and Mary sees that none of his food has been touched. He is moving slowly side to side, his rigid, little body showing how tired he is, and Mary works to calm him. Stinker relents, out of pure exhaustion no doubt, and permits Mary to carry and rub what must be stiff legs as she walks to the living area. Light as a feather, the thin-limbed child distresses Mary, who repeats like a comforting chant, "My poor little boy, my little boy."

Mary is the one woman of the family without a child, and the women watch her gently try to bend Stinker's knees so he can sit. Unsuccessful, Mary gives up and leans Stinker against her while she sits. He does not allow touching now, but Mary may stroke the hem of his tee. She is grateful to touch him via his tee.

Satisfied that Stinker, in his way, is among them, the women return to their work while someone absently flicks on the TV remote. A horrid news story blasts about a mother who binds her baby with duct tape, kills her, and leaves her little body in the woods. The women stop in their tracts and collectively gasp at the dreadfulness of the crime. The air movement in the room stops in disbelief. How could a woman not want her baby?

Maxi, still with her gifts, protectively puts her arms across her belly. Her knees buckle, and her mask fades. Her mother and Godmother rush to her. Mary, visibly shaken and bracing Stinker, tries to push a chair over with one hand. Barbara and others help Maxi to a chair, Godmother lowers her head, Barbara rubs her back, and Ally pats her hand while Martha fans. The children hush, Aunt Mary and Stinker seem to slide nearer to Maxi, and Godmother orders the TV off.

"Shocking a mother-to-be!" she reprimands everyone.

The women surround Maxi, give words of encouragement, tell her the best times to eat to avoid nausea, assure her she will be a good mother, and give her vitamin advice. Hot tea with honey and some lightly buttered toast appear, as ordered by Godmother.

Little sister Becky stands silently watching big sister, with her furry pink handbag and Bratz dolly in hand. Becky is as intense as any woman in the room, absorbing, as if in a training session, on call if needed. She watches Stinker leaning on Aunt Mary's back as she feeds bits of toast to Maxi, and Barbara blows on each spoon of honey tea that Maxi must finish according to Mother and Godmother. She practices the same motions with her dolly. Maxi's beautiful mask of pregnancy returns, and a sigh of relief erupts from all.

Stinker stops leaning and becomes agitated again, moving side to side. Mary's caressing of his tee no longer stills him. Attentive eyes move from Maxi to Stinker. The women huddle around Maxi and the unborn baby. Does Stinker sense something? His frail collarbone and ribs show through his tee, his eyes are fluttering, the child's breath is waning, and the women are afraid and hold their breaths with him.

God, protect your little one, Mary's eyes begs to heaven, beyond the ceiling, and Godmother shouts aloud for the angels to surround this sweet lamb with no voice. The women move closer to Stinker. Ally holds Maxi's hand tightly for fear she may suffer another fright. Martha does not leave her daughter's side.

Mary softly speaks to Stinker, repeatedly. "Stay with us, stay with us." The silence of the women is like a prayer. His spirit returns, and he stirs but is too weak to stand. He sits between Mary's legs on the floor.

Becky, without prompting, goes and gets a big glass, fills it with vanilla ice cream, and pours orange soda pop in. She leaves her bag and dolly behind on the table. Repeatedly, she tries to spoon-feed Stinker. Godmother stands by as if her presence will force Stinker to hang on.

Newspapers are brought in and put under Stinker in case he messes himself. In her child voice, Becky repeats, "Stinker, stay with us. Stinker, we love you. Stay."

Stay, the women whisper in their hearts.

After many patient attempts, Stinker finally swallows, and the women of the family keep their vigil.

The telephone rings, but no one moves.

"Maybe it's his mama," Mary says gently.

Bull, standing in the shadows for some time, in awe of the bond and love the women of the family freely share, quietly moves to answer the phone, as Godmother with a nod, bids him to do, and Stinker stills.

American Blue Eyes

(Iran/Iraq War-A Day In '88)

Propelling my unbalanced pregnant self nearer to the door, in instinctual mode, waddling faster, I retrieve Fatimeh's and my black street chadors, and grab flip-flops and my bag, which is packed with everyone's national ID cards, ration coupons, other documents, a few meds, and an eyeliner pencil, my last token of vanity. Edging closer to the exit, tense calf muscles sense the siren before it warns terror is approaching. War does that. It hones long lost survival skills. Your legs know "fight or flight" the same as animals know to move before the first shake of an earthquake. Other women have mentioned that they, too, move before the air raid siren blares.

The siren goes off just as I reach the door, almost in consideration of my condition. I scream for Mehdi and Fatimeh to come by me immediately. I stopped using their Anglican names long ago; the schools and family made it an issue. My name is not my own either. Moving with reluctance from the near-collapsed cellar they've been sitting in, enjoying its relative coolness, they fear my mother bear roar as much or more than the siren, and run up the stairs, knowing full well we will be running down them again. *Play it safe* rolls in my head. *Remain calm. You know the drill.* My only real adult company is the gray matter in my head. These internal conversations are nonstop, and the words stay only with me.

His father has warned our son, of course, "Mother is pregnant, therefore overanxious and mental." Mehdi is the man of the house in his father's absence and is to supervise mom and older sister, and report. *What if the women get mental?* the poor boy must fear. The internal self protests smartly, bravely but without sound. Only if my husband is a mind reader does he know these words. *Bullshit, your Royal Highness. Exactly what is the boy to report? Half the time, I'm racing round trying to track where he's off to!* You lose your will to challenge even in your head after a while though.

"Sirens and warnings are always sounding, and we're not dead yet … Soooo, Mom, why the panic? It's too hot to huddle in stairwells," the kids moan.

"The TV says we have to!" I shout with authority. After all, the TV is government controlled and war announcements are every day. "We'll go to that post office shelter you guys hate if you answer me back," is my reply. The electricity is four hours on and four hours off, the same with the water of late. I'm thinking of dinner and the wash instead of concentrating on the fact that zero dinner or wash remain if hit, and it astounds me.

It's better to be bombed during the day, they discuss in their father's native tongue, Farsi, knowing I understand more than I let on. Right, of course; the necessary blackouts during the night heighten the terror. My entire body tenses at the thought of night air raids.

School teaches us it's a glory to be a martyr. They continue in this vein just to get my goat. "A kid's job is to live," is my sharp answer back. There's logic for the best time of the day for martyrdom of children? I swirl this position in the secret crevices of my skull and consider grandmother's adage—you're to clear the swamp, not wrestle the alligators—and hold my tongue. I've been away from home so long, I wonder if I remember it correctly. Pregnancy does make one mental about keeping your child alive, however.

"Do as you are told!" I shout in English. Their eyes repent, if I read them right. It's easier to join the flow, be seduced by the rhetoric, and believe not as your home culture taught, if only to hold the peace in your own house. I add to the children's confusion, I realize. Even to gather loved ones in one spot during a raid is nonsensical; it means all perish from the missile.

If his father were home, my man-child would run to the roof and shout in cadence, "Allah Akbar, death to Israel, death to America, death to Saddam!" and whatever new enemy the state designates death to in order to foster morale. War drains the lifeblood of a country, literally, and the enemy may cross the border in hours. You can see which side of the city is hit better of course. You know how near the disaster is to you from a rooftop, but ears hear as much, my brain says. However, maybe it's less fearful to actually see what happens. I don't know. Women remain indoors in this household with their minds to judge where the attack is.

Reading the eyes of the other women in the building is difficult. Do they hate their sons on the rooftops like I do? Do they have secret thoughts? Am I alone? What am I thinking? I'm just a part of the mess like them. I join the women in the streets as trucks hauling bodies of slain soldiers slowly wind through city streets. The wailing, the worry, the grief of whose son, husband, family is in a box hangs in the polluted air long after the trucks pass. I hate Saddam as loudly as they do, share rumors about rations and the warfront news when I get it. After all, I am a foreigner and can listen and understand other news reports, they often remind me. I have no access to any information, of course. Complex Farsi is beyond my abilities; to sit through a long-winded dissident report would be beyond my understanding.

The women tease me that I'm an American blue-eyed devil with two young devils and another one on the way. I put up with it; both kids have American blue eyes. However, they do have their father's dark hair and his sister's nose, I point out. I'm tapping my belly, thinking about the eye color of the little one inside. How do you live with a family and not live with them?

Moving down the stairs, mind afire, any number of unrelated events flash in my head. The family funeral for Mohammad, only fifteen, tortured in an Iraqi prison camp, plays in my head like a movie as we speed down the stairs. His mama identified his skinny body by his underwear, newly purchased for him before he left. The little verse from the Koran sewn in his undershirt that was to comfort and protect; she clings to it. I threw myself on the parlor rug weeping for the boy. What kind of devils torture a boy, a boy too shy to look me in the eye, a boy whose mama buys proper, modest long shorts for, a boy who never kissed a girl? I fill with guilt at being an American. After all, does not the media say every day it's our fault? *Move feet. For God's sake!*

The women wail the high-pitch yodel for the dead; I am choking, unable to be loud enough. I'm crazy with grief for a boy I hardly knew. I'm boiling mad at the boy's mama and daddy for signing the permission form that let him to go to war. I want to kill Saddam. I'm enraged at my husband, Washington, and the whole fucking world.

The mother is pounding her head and chest, pulling out her hair, and I join her. The women put cold water on me. I'm hysterical. I've stepped into an insane maze I can't find my way out of. Am I a closet mourner? Do I belong to them and not know it? The anguish, the grief, is overwhelming. My flip-flops sound as I move more rapidly, with each boom, down the stairs with the children. Who am I? How do I think of such things during an air raid?

No men about—just me, the kids, baby, and the woman upstairs with her children, and she's pregnant too. I run through my head what "they" expect me to do. My father-in-law is at the mosque, and the children's father has gone on a trip no less! I'm happy for this absence of men—except for the air raid and panic going on, that is.

My brain doesn't know when to be happy anymore. "Move! Run!" I shout aloud for my own benefit.

My daughter and I are veiled and waiting on our landing with our bags as we hurry our neighbor, running down her flight of stairs. She is hanging on to her son. Her daughter, though not nine, knows her place and is in full veil. All the windows have large strips of masking tape. Huge Xs are everywhere. The stairwell faces the street; therefore, frosted windows are required. The kitchen, bathroom, all areas where the women work, you can't see out of. Walls surround and hide us in the patio area. An outside toilet, a water source, the men's motorbikes, gas capsules, grills, and any number of tools are only a few of the things hidden. Frosted windows are to make us comfortable, protect us from prying eyes, but I once lived in wide-open prairie spaces. The protection makes me paranoid, makes me feel helpless and isolated. Pregnancy hormones weaken one and make for anti-revolutionary thought, I am told. My problem is Western me-ism, in-laws have informed me.

Angry brain cells answer back to the charge of "Westernism." Logic supports me. The enemy is at the border, we are all going down, and we're only at the second landing. We race in a pack, but compared to missiles, we run in slow motion. Another huge boom shakes the air. My heart literally quivers and misses a beat. Someone is dead and gone forever with that boom. That's what that sound means. *Run!*

More booms. Closer, moving with precision, the war monster is stomping our way, filled with hate. The big guns on the post office roar back, firing one after another, and sonic booms follow. Aircrafts move faster than children's legs. Explosions are nearer, louder, louder. I'm having a hard time breathing, moving faster, and my neighbor is panting. We just hit the first landing. We must get under the stairwell.

Am I having an attack of hives? My lip is swelling. The kids are pulling us mothers now. I'm having an allergic reaction to war. I laugh aloud at my mind's rambling. My son frowns. Do hives bleed, or has something hit my face? My daughter is staring at my lip. One flip-flop is gone.

They are bombing our section of the city. I don't hear the comforting anti-aircraft guns on the post office sound. I'm having trouble catching my breath. Shortages of ambulances ... doctors sent to the front ... motorcycles ... ordinary cars commandeered to bring bodies home ... a river full of bodies ... boys in the water ... civilians commanded to remain brave ... prepare for hand-to-hand combat ... cover your faces in case of poison gas attacks ... my head is swirling with directions and orders.

God damn it. We didn't bring weapons, wet cloths, or bandages with us. My eyes pop at the kerosene cans under the stairwells. That's dangerous. If a missile hits, we'll go up in flames with them stored there. What am I thinking? If a missile hits us, we will all be part of a hole in the ground. Only a few bones, trinkets, and ashes will remain. I am afraid for my baby. My neighbor holds her belly too. We practically sit on our children. My son, as is her son, is itching to see out the front door. I hold tight to the back of my boy's shirt. He has me to drag with him if he leaves, but he does not pull away from me this time. The sound is deafening.

My neighbor is moving away from the stairwell, going near frosted glass on the entrance door. She is begging her father-in-law to come down and sit with us. What? Am I hearing right? The old idiot! She is using the usual respectful terms you use to speak to your husband's family. The booms are louder, and she cannot shout loud enough to cover the din.

"He can't hear you," I try to tell her. Mehdi is older than her boy. Sending him might be an option, as no woman in my family is permitted to touch him because of religious law. How is a twelve-year-old to drag him down if he doesn't want to come, however? What if the old man sends Mehdi to the roof to check things out? We yell together for the old man to come down.

In the Moment

He can't hear. If by some remote chance he can hear, the old man still refuses to come down. A small lull in the den allows us to finally hear him yell from the apartment door. "I'm old. I climbed four flights of stairs to get up here. Stop screaming!" He continues, "Weak one," how old-timers address their women, "I want my tea! Whatever Allah wants!"

Am I the one mad? Hell no! Why does God want this? I want to tell the old fart to move his butt down the stairs this second, but I don't dare. I cannot offend.

A fast whooshing sound—I smell it go by. A great fireball passes; it is a missile. Closing my eyes to avoid seeing the devil riding its back, I cross myself in front of all and scream the same time my neighbor does. All faiths recognize evil.

The children have absorbed our terror, and their mouths appear to be screaming with us. The detonation is so loud, the neighbor's mouth moves, but her words are silent. Our hands cover one child's ears and then the next. We do not have enough hands. Did the missile hit the nursery school in the city park? Two windows on the upper floors shake loose and fall to the street, but I don't hear it; I know it happened by the full sunlight streaming in. I sense people running, shouting. A mountain of dust is rising, but from where? How will I sweep it all?

The old man comes down the stairs, appears to order his daughter-in-law in the house as he scowls at me. I ask his forgiveness, as custom requires, but it doesn't seem like anyone has hearing, and the old man is not wearing his hearing aids. Moving from rote, like programmed robots, we rise. What did I need a kitchen knife for? I seem to remember needing one.

The neighbor's father-in-law knows I'm a foreigner, and he doesn't like any of his family to be near me. Maybe he's Hezbollah, maybe he just wants his tea, or maybe the propaganda against foreigners in general causes him to shun me. Maybe my ambiguity is obvious—you're either for or against—or maybe his ears hurt and he's scared too.

My neighbor and I help each other up the stairs and slowly follow behind her father-in-law. The kids seem a little crushed, shocked. They seem shorter. "How are your ears?" I ask repeatedly.

I want to embrace my neighbor, but maybe her eyes were open when I made the sign of the cross. Unclean, an infidel, my touch may offend. Her eyes are glazed with terror, and she doesn't need trouble. Her father-in-law is waiting. She climbs the stairs on all fours. After bombings, legs work as badly as the Strawman's in *The Wizard of Oz*.

I can't do the stairs with two legs either, but I need to get behind my door, in my frosted world. Too exhausted to think, to move, my mind between two worlds is draining. It saps my energy. Is the baby kicking? I move my belly. *Kick, baby.* Mehdi's face is covered with dust. I brush, dust him off as he helps me into the apartment. Fatimeh is dusty too. I try to flap her chador, but she pulls away and shakes her veil at the door, to track as little dust into the apartment as possible. Dust is seeping in through cracks in the doors and windows. A big building collapsed very near. Mehdi keeps rubbing his ears.

We flop on the floor, spent, but we all wonder where the bomb hit. Mehdi fidgets, wants to go see where the bomb hit. I don't actually hear him asking, and *not enough hands for all the ears* runs through my head uselessly. I warn Mehdi shrilly to return immediately if the siren goes off. "I can't get to the hospital on my own," I whine. Why am I so dependent? Everyone is near tears. Fatimeh speaks to me while I rub my ears. Her sounds are words under water. I can't make them out. I am so thirsty; they must be too.

"I can get you a cab," Fatimeh asserts with an angry face, if I read her lips right. Mehdi is on his feet, up to leave, and promises to return. I gather this from his gestures. Is he mocking his sister and me? No, he's a good boy. He would have to be our escort; we would be in the way, and I would stand out with my American blue eyes and thick accent. If someone we know, family or a neighbor, died in the attack, Mehdi will have to sit in the mourning room with the men. In the next room, he will hear the mad cries of the women for the lost. Defeated, what can I say? He's right; we are not merely observers of the war.

Fatimeh sits silently with her own dark thoughts. I look at the tape on the frosted windows, seeing cracks everywhere. The wait for electricity will be a long one. Both of us eye the broom; one of us should use it on the stairs. Instead, I stretch out my legs on the floor and rest my back on the carpet pillow my dear daughter brings. She puts her head on what little lap and legs I have to spare for her, bracing the baby to come.

Waiting anxiously for Mehdi, ten years from now has no meaning to me. Life is this moment, and I can hardly bear it.

Back Issue

Contemplating the computer screen, a warm puff of air brushes my neck, reminding me of how it tickled when you kissed me behind the ears and gently pulled on my earlobes with your mouth—earrings and all—so long ago. No matter how angry I was at the time, an involuntary smile would come, and you would laugh and say, "See how much you still love me."

Pulling a yellowed, torn shade down to the windowsill, on make-do beds, I would lick your nipples, politely kiss and suck your penis, and relish your sigh of pleasure. A little wild then, now hinted at or seen in movies today, we were such children. The sun would pour around the sides of the shade and create a soft, yellow-red glow in the room that no wall paint could duplicate. It softened all the edges away.

Apartment décor was mattresses on the floor, with hand-sewn throw pillows and a poster of Janis Joplin with a boa on the wall. The radiators we painted traffic-sign yellow, which the landlord demanded we make silver again. Our ceiling was dark blue with stars. Growing up, neither of us had our own rooms or parents that indulged much, which explains a lot, I guess. The Salvation Army was the store of choice for clothes, shoes, wonderful summer hats, and furniture back then. I reinvented whatever we bought. Meals consisted of spaghetti, sweets, and wine.

At seldom paid-for movies, we thought nothing of publicly feeling each other up, and french kissing was a gift for all to see. We would discreetly wipe our mouths after each deliberately provocative kiss, though. A telltale sign of our basic Puritanism, no doubt. Downtown, we strolled dressed like hippies, sometimes asking for change to buy our smokes or ride the bus. We were against "the man" and not into the forty-hour-plus workweek grind. Young, we thought we were originals, the first and only ones who defied the rules.

We worked hard to be a sign of the times. We knew the words that agitated, the dances that insinuated, and the drugs that hallucinated. At anti-war demonstrations, we stayed on the fringes though, grateful that flat feet prevented a tour of duty in Vietnam for you. Bail would have been difficult anyway, but we respected Joan Baez's husband and the Chicago Seven and their like when they went to prison.

Pot smoking did not help me in the typing pool, nor were you into bagging at the A&P. It seemed logical to head to San Francisco. Sleeping in airports and the cool of parks was possible then, if you moved enough. There were free stores, and food was available. We survived on little, but those kids in San Francisco were not us. We were more cynical, working class, too Midwestern, used to hard winters. We hitchhiked home.

Social conventions were creeping into our psyches. Overnight, free love seemed passé. A new adulthood emerged, as did safe sex. The world was dancing a new way, and the word "unfaithful" took back its old meaning. Wanting to be the head typist, I began to go to work on time, every day, without fail.

We did not ask for change on the subway anymore. You bought a car and wore your hair in a neat ponytail. Getting stoned became infrequent. You bought car insurance, and I purchased underwear from Sears. Incense bothered our eyes now, for some reason. A woman showed up at the door holding a little boy with your exact same eyes, and the leaving began.

You called for a while, missed me, still loved me, but ... Returning to the Church, sin was back with me. We lost touch completely. Marriage, kids, work, divorce, others, and old age followed.

If I calculate correctly, 1,576,800 minutes or more were spent thinking about you, doping with you, sexing with you, loving you, but who counts three years that way? Except my stupid heart, that is. *Those days we can never retrieve, and how real are memories some thirty-five years old?* my common sense correctly asks. *Memories seen through rose-colored glasses.*

The mirror shows a thick midriff, flabby arms, and thinning, colored gray hair. The medicine chest is full of doctor-prescribed dope. I am a "back issue," as Mother described herself when her youth was spent.

Was it the era that made us lovers, or was it bigger, something more? My heart begs the question. Facebook and the like are all part of life now, a brave new world, and whatever and whomever you want is out there; just press "enter."

The computer waits patiently for my timid heart to dare.

A Spinning Top

Miss Towers is using her usual loud voice as she reads straight from a teaching manual. Her manner and tone are not her usual Coach ones, however. Heavyset, short hair parted to the side, chipped red-painted nails, Coach is different from the other women teachers. Comfortable in her elastic-legged, ancient bloomer shorts we girls hate to wear, she often trots in the hallways wearing baggy trousers and what look to be men's sweaters. We respect her, love her even, and many of the boys admire her too. She is religious but punishes without meanness. Our eighth-grade gym teacher/choir director/recess monitor is the new sex education instructor for the girls now.

"Rape is today's topic for discussion," she announces. It is like an air raid siren going off, and it's not Tuesday. We are surprised. Hold yourself to avoid penetration. Be passive. The man will relent, and you will have a better chance at survival. Remember, you can provoke an attack on your person by improper dress and manner of behavior with the opposite sex. Watch how you cross your legs, tuck your arms behind your skirt when bending, the color of your bra under a white blouse is of importance, and never let your straps show. Rape prevention is possible if you are careful. Do not go out alone or unescorted at night, walk in the middle of the sidewalk, never drink alcohol at bars, always say your prayers. She is not reading word for word from the teaching manual as she did with the other issues. Miss Towers looks us each in the eye. She speaks like an auntie, "Submit to rape to save your life, if you must." Coach is giving us a direct order.

Sex education class is objectionable to our parents, and a petition to end the class is in circulation. Open discussion of such matters is "disgusting." The information from the menstrual cycle pamphlet is late for more than half of the girls in class, though I read it as told. Information on marital relations is a bigger joke. The leaflet does not explain anything about intercourse that seems useful. There is nothing technical on how to do it or how it feels, and it is sin, so how will we ever know what to do? I pretend a nonchalant attitude as the other girls do, but I have seen and heard enough in my life to understand that the class is important. It just doesn't go far enough.

It is 1960, and we eighth-grade girls wear skirts to school and like nothing better than hanging around and sharing forbidden lipsticks and eyeliners at recess. We write letters to one another and pick out better names for ourselves than our parents did. We know the top ten radio hits by heart and practice singing them and dance with each other. Spin the bottle is something some of us have played at birthday parties, and I have kissed three boys so far. None of us have had sex yet, but I have a cousin who married at fourteen. I joke that I must find a husband soon. We want to grow up, the sooner the better.

Dodge ball is not a favorite sport among us girls, for a reason. A certain male teaches has it in for us "lazy" girls. He deliberately pits the boys against the girls. He insists the boys kick the ball hard at the girls to "make them move." The teacher leads and plays with the boys against the girls. Some of the boys don't want to play with the girls, period. Two boys defy the teacher and warn certain girls they like that the ball is coming, or throw the ball high against the wall. Eyeglasses are not plastic. Two of the girls fear the "nice" boys as well. Glasses cost money; a parent might blame the girl. The results are always the same of course. We lose. To move fast, jump higher, or run is almost impossible for us. We have to contend with the modesty issues of skirts we must hold on to, and flats that slip off and limit movement. Black and blue marks on ankles and calves are the only tangible lesson in sportsmanship we receive.

Sometimes if a girl falls, our Miss Towers shows up "out of the blue." She orders us to play ladylike and turn rope for the younger girls. She is odd but protects us, we realize. This particular male teacher gives us the creeps.

There are mean boys and men who enjoy hurting females. Some of our mothers, aunties, and neighbors play a dodge ball of sorts, I observe. Like Coach, they caution us not to "set off" the men.

Zigzag running, keys in the eyes, kicks to the groin, a weapon on your person, and screaming are not included in rape-prevention recommendations. Self-defense training for women is unheard of, DNA testing unknown, and women's lib is but a whisper. Women police wear skirts. Fast-forward five, six years: "rape" and "submission" are still linked actions. Reporting a rape puts you at risk of being "eaten alive" in court. Is Miss Towers aware that her working-class girls are finished with school, work now, take the bus, and seldom have someone to escort them home?

Coming home from work in the later sixties, I am grabbed a short distance from my bus stop. The winter darkness and cold, a broken streetlamp, and a cumbersome ankle-length coat make it easy for him to grab me from behind. He holds me tight around the throat with one arm and wraps his other arm around my chest. He is much taller than I am, and I literally dangle as he picks me up to get a better grip while I struggle. Strangely, I remember a premonition on the bus. I sensed I should get off at the next stop, go farther and backtrack, but I was dead tired. I beat myself over the head many times about this premonition ignored.

My attacker threatens to kill me if I give him trouble; he has a gun and swears he'll use it. He is hurting me. No one is on the sidewalk, and no car turns off the main street. If I "be good," I will enjoy myself. "We will party," he states with confidence. He jabs me in the back with his gun, but it feels sharp like a knife. He is choking me with his heavy arm, and it is natural to squirm. He makes me feel like an errant child when he shakes me for moving. I try to kick his ankle, missing; I can't move in this coat. He takes his arm off my throat but is still holding me around the chest when I hear duct tape tear. I panic, fighting, crying, and yelling without much sound as he struggles to wrap the tape around my mouth and head. He punches me hard to the head, woozy; to remain conscious is an effort. A car passes but does not see. I am limp as he pushes me into his car and spins away from the curb. He rips two buttons off my coat, shaking me more. He screams for me to shut up. I'm not talking; I can't talk with the duct tape. The tears are making him mad.

Lectures from eighth-grade sex education move around in my head. I am wrapped head to toe for winter. What did I do wrong? I try the door. (Seat belts are not required.) We are not to the highway yet; maybe I can jump out and escape. The door opens, but my assailant is fast and pulls me back in. He punches me so hard in the chest I lose my breath. I am "asking for it" now. He stops dead in the middle of the street, grabs my wrists, and duct tapes them behind me. Flooring the gas pedal, he speeds off and turns into a little forest preserve area not far from where he seized me.

"Get out!" he shouts, so full of rage at me. I stand meekly outside the car waiting for him to shoot me. He merely gets out of his side of the car. I remain frozen. "Walk, you little idiot." The deeper snow makes it hard to move. I fall, and he begins to help me walk.

Still crying softly and having trouble breathing, in "frustration" from dealing with me, he rips the duct tape off my mouth and head. The tape tears off pieces of my chapped lips, making them bleed, and an involuntary yelp comes out as the tape pulls on my long hair. As we trudge, I am grateful to breathe easier.

I say nothing but continue having trouble keeping up. With his penknife, he cuts the tape from my hands. It is less effort for him to pull me along by my arm. "Be good. I won't hurt you if you be good," he repeats several times. "I'll be good." I say it because I don't know what else to say. Feeble, dizzy, and cold, I ask God in my head to save me, protect me.

We are in a secluded area, and it is snowing again. As if awoken from a dream, I realize he is ripping at my coat. Crying, pleading, my stupor ends. "Do you think I want a walk in the snow with you?" he laughs. Shocked back to reality, I raise my hand, but with one hard shove from him, I fall in the snow. He will rape me.

Regular but large features, blond curly hair, his breath reeks of liquor and cigarettes. He is kissing me. The fight is knocked out of me; still I turn away. Having a problem getting my air up, my legs strain to remain closed, tights and panties pulled off, bare feet in the snow; I try to hold myself to prevent penetration. It happens anyway.

The forced sex act does not last long. It hurt, but worse is the humiliation and disgust flooding me; I blush. I feel shame warming my face, I feel beet red. He lights a cigarette and pulls me up by my coat, throwing my boots at me. To be left in the snow is all I want.

Swearing as he drags me back to the car, he yells for me to stop looking at him. Shoving me in the car, he takes a flask from the dashboard, takes a swig, and orders me to drink. I sip the cold liquor slowly, politely even. Enraged at me for what I do not know, he rapes me again in the car. A ragdoll that does not whimper or say a word does not suit him either. A tirade of horrible, mean words follow, but it lulls my ears. I prefer his hateful words to his touch.

He takes a large screwdriver from his coat. Brandishing it with a self-satisfied laugh, he says, "See, I don't have a gun." Waving the screwdriver in my face, "I had you twice because you thought I had a gun." Laughing louder, he says, "Look! I only have a pocketknife, not a street blade! The joke's on you, sister. If you tell anyone, I'll kill you. I mean it. I know where you work and where you live." I feel dead, a tiny ash that will blow away any moment. He stops laughing, starts the car, and drives slowly out of the parking lot. He is thinking what? I shudder

Silent suddenly, he drives me back to the bus stop, opens the door, and pushes me out. Standing on the curb meekly, I wait for him to pull away. Instead of going to my little basement apartment, I cross the street and catch a bus to my mother's house. Few are on the bus this late, but all eyes are on me. I wrap my coat more tightly.

In the entryway, Mother wants to know why I've come so late and why I look a mess. I blurt out I need to call the police. The ash resurrects; I know I did nothing wrong! "What have you done? Why come here to call the cops? What is wrong?" Mother continues all in one breath. With shock, I realize my underpants and tights must still be in the woods; the long coat is my only friend. As I tell mother what happened, grief, anguish, disgust, and fear dance in her eyes, quiver on her lips, and move to her shoulders and back. She slumps and becomes small in her chair, almost as small as me.

The police arrive and begin grilling me. They want details, complete descriptions of the sex act. Was I on a date, did I know him, how many sexual partners I had, the questions went on and on. Mother sits quietly smoking cigarette after cigarette. I want to pull my coat over my head. Finally, the police need to know if I took a bath, and if not, do I want to press charges? If so, I have to go to St. Mary's to verify that I am telling the truth.

The cops stand in the examination room at my head—talking shop as a hospital doctor probes me. I struggle through my first pelvic exam. Though I have a lover, I am unmarried and therefore never dealt with a gynecologist before. I feel my face reddening. The nurse mentions that I'm having trouble breathing, but the doctor concludes it is stress and a sedative will calm me. A light brush of her hand to my shoulder causes tears to slide into my ears. No picture is taken of my lips, wrists, or body. The police take the doctor's report in hand, which states that there is evidence of sexual intercourse and minor injuries.

Released from the hospital, the beat cops take me directly to the station to look at mug shots. Repeatedly, they ask the same questions. They need details. Why didn't I know he had a screwdriver and not a gun, was I on a date, did I come on to him, and do I enjoy sex? Will I still press charges? Sometimes they wrote what I said and sometimes not. The sedative is overwhelming me; I can barely keep awake. A policewoman walks by me twice. Does she think I'm lying? She walks to another desk and speaks to an officer in a suit. The questions keep coming. Was I a fool to report this? I feel nauseous, so weak. Still I pick my rapist from the books of pictures.

The plainclothes detective that the policewoman spoke with walks toward me with authority. He announces I am to go home and will be "interviewed" more later. It is difficult for me to stand on my own two feet, but one of the cops questioning me manages to get me home.

Waking up late the next morning on my unopened pull-out bed, still wearing my long coat and boots, I jump to call work and make some excuse about why I can't come in. Sitting down again, numb for a time longer, alone and sick to my stomach, I head to the bathroom to bathe. While undressing, I spot bruises on my shoulder and chest. My face and lip are swollen. The medicine cabinet shows only the half of it. As the water fills the tub, I notice a cut on my knee, my foot has a scratch, and a mark is on the inside of my upper thigh. I have been battered. Everything comes back to me as I sit in the tub. Rage at my rapist, self-hatred, disappointment with family and the system, helplessness begins to flood me. The water is cold. I hear the small radiator hiss and sputter, but the room is too cold and the water like ice. Yet I sit and continue to sit shaking until it is dark out.

A few days later, the detective rings and says looking at more mug shots and further "talking" is necessary. He picks me up and comments that I have not changed my story once yet, no matter how hard I was questioned, which is good. I relax a bit and pick the same man from his stack of mug shots, but the questioning begins anew. Do I know the guy is married with a family? *Am I to feel sorry that my rapist is a family man?* rushes through my head. He continues to type and question me, and laughs that he wishes I could type up the report for him.

"Should I have fought more?" is my question for him.

Looking me straight in the face, the detective says, "No, if he hit you when you obeyed, what do you think he would do if you didn't? You should see some of my cases where the girls put up a better fight than you did. You did good."

The "be good" of the rapist and the "did good" of the detective mix in my head as I am bombarded with more questions. The detective goes on, "Your attacker lives in the neighborhood. He has a record a mile long and several rape complaints filed that never made it to court. You're not the first one he's made trouble for. Help keep him off the streets for a while. You're right to report this. You've kept your wits about you." The idea of "good" still dances in my head as a beat cop assigned to me drives me home.

Terrified, "I have to go to work" is the excuse I use when informed my rapist is at the station. "A police soldier will pick you up," I am told. "This will go fast." I know my rapist, and I pick him out of the lineup instantly. Charges are filed, and a court date will be set is what I'm told. I promise to be there. "Please, I must get to work," I continue, drained and sad. My rapist is put in a chair not far from where I stand. He is given bond information. I just want to get out of there.

The trial date looms. Anxious and afraid, I now see my rapist on the street. He was always there; I just never noticed. I look for him now, see him in my dreams, and don't want to go to court alone. My boyfriend needs time to sort things out and fades away. No family member is available. I go over and over the details in my mind until I stop remembering.

In the Moment

A neighborhood friend agrees to drive me to court but has limited time to borrow his dad's car. Arriving for the arraignment, we see the court is full of roughnecks, cops trying to keep detainees in line, clashes. My timid driver is uncomfortable; he'll wait in the hall. My attacker I see immediately, with his pregnant wife in tow. His hair is short. He is cleaned up and whispers to his lawyer as he nods in my direction. The detective pops up beside me. I didn't realize I was holding my breath and gulped air in relief.

The court is noisy as the judge makes decisions in quick succession. The talking is faster and faster, and the room spins as my case is called. I can barely move, and I walk in slow motion. The court is eerily quiet. Charges are read; details are required. I am told to speak louder. The judge wants to know what the sexual positions were. I'm not sure what he means. Why did I comply if I did not see a gun? Why did I get off the bus where I did? Do you know this man? What were my injuries? The judge is handed a report. The same pattern of questions I had at Mother's, the police station, everywhere, but before a bigger audience. I freeze. Before I realize it, the case is dismissed; there is "not enough evidence to support a charge of rape." I can't process what is being said. Bewildered, I stagger and then flee.

The detective runs after me and wants to know what the matter is. "Why did you stop talking?" he yells. He wants to go back and challenge the decision. I am to wait right here, but I feel my head shaking no. I can't go in. I cannot go back in. I see my friend stand. Without a word, I run to the exit. I hear the detective slap his leg and scream, "Damn it to hell!" I am confused. Where is the car? Disoriented, my friend takes over and puts me in the car. I dissolve with my hands covering my face.

Entering his parent's home, he asks me, "Do you need a joint, a drink, something …" We light up on the back porch. I ask him if he thinks I'm a liar, if he wants sex; he doesn't is his response to both questions. Unsure, feeling worse, I thank him for the ride and leave to catch a bus home, knowing I'll never see him again on a regular basis.

I fall off the edge for a while, lose my boundaries, and lead an eventful life by anyone's standards, but life and the years pass, more than forty of them to be exact. One event cannot sum up a life. Friends and lovers come and fade, husbands leave, children, jobs, and other connections change. A blizzard of happenings, happy times, challenges, misfortunes, and illnesses change your perspective, take a toll.

Strangely, I never track my rapist or look for information about him. Maybe the nightmares are the reason. For a long time, I dreamed my rape as it happened, reliving every "mistake" I thought I made. Crying and afraid, I would wake. The dream changed as I did, after a while though. In the newer dream, I'm a dancer twirling and twirling over the snow without a heavy coat to drag me down, knowing there is danger ahead; I cannot stop the dance and move forward. Darker and darker, the dread is so real; it gets colder and colder. I am crying as the horror builds, but my brain knows where to wake me and stop the dream. I don't go back to sleep but let the TV make noise for me, so I don't feel alone.

Years pass, and his ghost seldom haunts my dreams; my protective brain cells see to that. One night, however, I find myself doing my dance again, twirling over snow, but I have changed. I dance like a furious spinning top, purposely rushing to the cold and dark, armed and ready to see him. Keys in my hand, I gouge at his eyes. Whirling faster and faster, fearlessly I remove my blade from my sleeve. An ice wind twisting, I plunge it into his throat. Without rancor, I tell him I will show him mercy. I have a gun and plan to use it; there is no "trick" he will have to explain later. Revolving on all sides around him, the spinning top I am is full of white-hot, unstoppable rage. I blur from the speed I've built up and shoot him dead. I howl triumphantly as blood colors the snow. Slowing, my heart wobbles momentarily at my hate, but I calm my body and spin myself back to sleep.

Rapture

The First Guard, the glimmering saints of old, like the tides of morn, gently laps close around the royal throne, washing it in adoration. In awe and reverence, a sacred wave of expectation gains momentum. Pure joy and admiration for the I AM build spontaneously. We are present, and in abiding peace with one another, a great sea of light, the atoned swirl in praise.

We recognize and love one another. Moreover, as we pass within one another, as we mingle, the spirit of one saint, glanced at in a passing moment, at a bus stop by another saint, is known and shared with the whole body. Each moment and life unrolls before and within us. A collective sigh for all those among us floats throughout the heavens, permeates each soul, adds further to the knowing. Thanks are to the I AM; there are no orphans, a universal language of knowledge prevails, all communication is possible. Feelings, words, sounds of humans, other creatures, first with I AM, the angels are implicit, distinguished and understood. The inclusion of many beliefs we comprehend and see the I AM's identity in them. The perfection of the hearts that the I AM created, we experience.

The delicate unborn are whole, strong, a crystal light, equal, glowing; they bubble brilliantly among us. The ages and ages of children harmed, their short lives a hell, are forever gathered and cradled by loving saints. The warmth of embraces make them sparkle and dart like bolts of lightning throughout the universes. So cherished are they; the souls are ecstatic to be with them. These young spirits leap freely throughout the compassionate hierarchy of the heavens. Dashing among the angels and other creatures, through the ranks they rush to the love that enfolds them.

Sin is conquered. Guilt, anguish, shame are nonexistent. Anxiety for tomorrow is eliminated; we are forever. No disheartened souls, never-to-be-abandoned, harmony and joy reign. Dominance is not desired, perfection in mind and body, flawless order; there is happiness.

The I AM approaches, and the rapture begins. All expectations will be met; everyone will have his full. Saints of old rush forward, up and still higher. More brilliant, their light shines, and like sheets and sheets of millions of waterfalls, their songs of praise ascend and pour. They expand and join repeatedly with other sounds and voices. The Body is like millions of tsunamis; huge waves of adoration climb. Universes from all times rise; those at the first day soar. The glory of the rapture, its beauty and truth, are repeated yet always changing, a grand holy mystery, expected, known and unknown. Individual souls within each tsunami leap, whirl, and twirl in ecstasy. Each member has a dance, a song, a gift of self to give to the I AM, yet the harmony is perfect. A divine sound rocks the uncountable. We swell to bursting. The passion flies to a grand crescendo of bliss, and all souls shake within.

The I AM meets and returns our love. No one is left out. Rising with each wave of saints, shaking in bliss, caressing us all, ever expanding, the I AM including, growing, loves us. We dance with and love our I AM; we join the Omnipresent. Blessedness, the dance, the intertwining make stupendous colors, sounds, and movements; paradise is complete. The feast of pure, perfect, never-ending love ensues; it is celebrated over and over. Each wave of rapture is new; we are more with every loving, satiated, whole; we see the face of I AM; we are alive!

Her Ex

How such a short-legged, chunky, sixtyish, "cut it myself" gray/red/brown-plaid-haired, loop-earring-sporting, more-than-loopy-looking, Hawaiian housedress-wearing woman can spring from a dead heap on my living room couch and sprint ahead of me to the front door is nothing short of a miracle!

"Mom, where do you think you're going?"

She sighs audibly, as if where she is going is an unknown.

"With you obviously, I'm going with you, naturally." She says this as she twirls full circle to get her fluffy arms into her coat.

Damn—she's out the door and padding down the slant sidewalk, huffing to the car in excitement, and worrying aloud about our run to the hospital. There's no choice. I use the keys to open the car doors and turn on the ignition. We are always the first ones called.

Man, I'm mad. I can't hold my tongue. "Mom, the man is your ex, and you're needed in the emergency room for what? Did he show for you two months ago? Are you nuts?" Spittle is frothing from my mouth; I am so agitated. He never runs for her.

She bristles and reminds me that her "ex" is my father. She continues to speculate what his medical situation is, how to best remedy it, and speculates if he has remembered to keep his supplemental insurance premiums up. I am fuming. She incites me further by stating she sees the smoke coming out of my ears.

"Who started the fire, Mom? Who?"

Pulling in the emergency driveway, I remind Mom not to jump out before the car stops. The ignition is off a second, and she churns into her take-charge mode, scooting out the door before me. We rush together through sliding doors and enter the packed waiting room area.

Unbelievable, but her appearance and good manners charm the emergency room staff, which grants her immediate attention and access to information. We know what curtain Dad is behind, and gobs of info hospital personnel don't necessarily hand out to exes. Not that she'd ever mention she was an ex. Mom's a work, but her thank-yous are never pretend.

Oh my God, Dad is bleeding from his mouth and nose, buckets of blood. He looks gray. Two nurses and a doctor are gathered about him. We are both aghast and crunch close to each other. My knees buckle, and Mom seats me before I hit the floor. Questions fly back and forth, all answered by Mom. She reminds me to take deep breaths and tells Dad, "It's nothing. They'll pack your nose, and you'll be out of here in an hour." Her nonsense chatter is somehow soothing to Dad and me. One of the nurses runs for something the doctor orders, and Mom holds a clamp thing on Dad's nose. His eyes turn often to her. Dad, forced to listen and unable to yell or dismiss her, actually seems calmed by her prattle. Blood is still coming out, however. Some is on Mom's shoe.

Concentrating on my rapid pulse, watching my father's face turn more ashen, I strain my eyes to focus on mother's carotid artery while imagining her galloping heart. I feel myself sliding from the chair. Mom takes me by the shoulders and tells me to go to the waiting room to look for my brother and sister, right now. Jell-O legs move as told.

Swaying into the nearest chair in the waiting room, glancing nauseously at the waiting sick, I text furiously. My brother, his wife, kids, baby sis, and her latest true love enter en masse and hover over me jokingly, finally distracting me from my texting.

"So, what's the news, big sis?" my brother slurs out as if we're all eating pizza and having beers! I blurt out in one breath that Dad is hemorrhaging to death and mother is near to a heart attack and what took everyone so long to get here. My sister-in-law looks at me darkly as she nods sideways to the kids.

Judging me hysterical, baby sister sucks her teeth and says, "Man, look who we're talking with. I'll check it out. Want to come look?" she coos authoritatively to the boyfriend. Brother follows sis, and my sister-in-law needs a smoke but will be in to see Dad directly. My jumping-without-reason nephews are left to render me moral support it appears.

I make every effort to compose myself while watching the kids, but within minutes, my brother, sister, and entourage reenter the waiting room, and any composure I have mustered leaves full speed.

"Dad looks like he's going down. Mom is crossing herself and looking to the ceiling for God!" my brother spills out, as his wife punches him in the arm and warns him with more sideway head movements about the kids. Sis seems to agree with brother's assessment of the situation. "You better get back in there," she states with emotion, as if I don't go in now, things will get worse, and it will be my fault.

I rush back. Mom is at her station, and blood is still gushing from Dad. Both of my parents seem to have blue lips. Is it poor blood circulation or the lighting? The room spins. Another doctor enters, and the staff working on Dad seems relieved. An additional IV bag is added to Dad's arm. Mom keeps telling him his color is improving as she shifts her weight on her legs. She's been standing longer than is good for her; she will not leave his side. She nods her approval at me, and I sit small so as not to be in the way, but to be there. Efforts to halt the bleeding continue.

The clock moves. The doctors and nurses rush back and forth, yet the whole room seems frozen; my brain can't process what is happening. The room only begins to melt when words like "stable and normal readings, have the balloon and packing removed in two days, an overnight stay is not necessary" float in the air. Mom finally sits down, pats my knee, and visibly shrinks, as some of the terror of the evening dances out of my chest.

Dad's color is better, and he states he'll stay at my brother's; Mother thinks that is a good idea. I wait for a special thank-you to Mom from him, but it never comes. My brother enters, chatters about the boys with Dad, says not to worry, everything is "copasetic," and the light talk about nothing continues as Mother breathes the smallest sign of relief that no one feels but me. We are dismissed with waves and kisses, as if we were nice guests who came for a short visit. I feel used.

Mom and I walk silently, and I literally put her in the car. I have no energy to point out to her the basic rejection from a man she obviously cares for. We ride in a car filled with fumes of exhaustion.

Mom finally asks if I can get her a diet soda pop and some Hostess Snowballs; she hasn't had her meds yet. Without judgment or pity, I pull into the gas station. "Should I get Lotto tickets, Mom?" She nods and rests her head on the window. The air outside is heavy, just like in the car. Her sorrow follows, and I carry it on my back with me into the station as I buy the goodies and the Lotto tickets that don't win us a thing.

Mom gulps down her heart pills and whatnot with the cold pop and hands me a Snowball Cupcake, almost as a penance for me putting up with her. "I know it doesn't make any sense, baby, I know," she says so timidly any anger I have evaporates. We just enjoy our cupcakes.

My heart and I understand unreturned love. It chips away at you, and nothing seems to make it better. I'm an ex too.

The Wedding

Hair teased, coifed, and sprayed profusely into a proper helmet, with old-fashioned spit curls on the side, completes my old-lady do for the biggest party in my daughter Angelina's life—her wedding. Daughter-in-law Katherine is in charge of the squad's beautification process. Early appointments helped little, as the beauty operators are behind. Customers with difficult hair, bad weather, and two dryers not working all contribute to the delay in this operation. Sloppy brinkmanship!

The ranking cosmetician is layering pink shadow on the eyelids of Katherine. Negative is the opinion of trained cosmetician. I am assured that silver eyelids are "appropriate, perfect, not overdone," and therefore, I endure the silver and anticipate passing inspection at this grand operation. It may prove an issue, if upon blinking of the eyes, the itchy, silver powdered substance applied, glows in the dark.

This wedding is a strategic military operation. Our squad's assignment is to, upon beautification of its two female members, return to temporary base (i.e., my son Thomas's townhouse), collect remaining members of squad, and proceed with all speed to reception hall area. Thomas, official rank of "bride-giver-a-wayer," and "ring-bearer" ranked Chris, grandson of this soldier and designated "sweetie-pie," are vital members of our squad. Finally,

Great-Grandpapa, the remaining member of the squad, will function as the "oldest family member of wedding party." Upon completion of last-minute inspection protocols, we will as a unit, move out in full bridal regalia and unite with other members of bridal regiment for formal picture taking, in the wedding hall. Picture duty complete, we proceed, in order, to reception area. Roger. Any deserters, stragglers, malcontents will face full disciplinary measures for any disruptions of this paramount photography session and/or reception party. Our cell is on full alert.

Platoons of in-laws and outlaws, out-of-state guests, and other contributing parties are in formation. Charming behavior is required of all participants before, during, and after event. We are to contribute to the peace, and the open bar is no excuse for infractions and ballyhoo. The bride, the commanding four-star general, with commander-in-chief delusions, will tolerate no lack of attention to details; this will be a transforming "shock and awe" event. Spit and polish rules the day. We will rise from working class to upper middle class. This wedding, no matter the costs or body count, will aspire to and exceed reality show weddings on cable TV. Victory is ours! Oorah!

Arriving at our base of operations, beautification near completion, daughter-in-law and self discover a situation is in progress. We observe that male members of primary squad are not showered and uniformed. Given repeated notifications during our beautification process, the male members of unit have not followed orders. Appearances show they have seen fit to only sit together and watch cartoons. They are alarmingly unmoved by the gravity of the situation and unconscious of precious time passing. This dereliction of duty causes Katherine and self to mead out intense verbal reprimand.

A fuming commanding general calls during reprimand. Reiterating that time is of the essence, she is hysterical. Arrival of wedding photographer is imminent. Members of groom's family are on premises. Armed with this information, elimination of showers for the aforementioned derelicts is deemed necessary. Direct attention to dress is indicated. This soldier gives the order to move with all speed.

Setting an example, to encourage immediate compliance with dress procedures, I race to the upstairs bedroom. Maneuvers are initiated to stuff gut and other body parts into my "all in one" armor-type underwear to achieve maximum spot lifting and tucking of the body. The mother of the bride's "chic and tasteful" two-piece gold ensemble is now on my person, as specified and ordered personally by General Angelina. Regrettably, weight gain appears to contribute to some spillage and puffing of body fat. Duly noted, and for optimal ascetic results, this soldier will consent only to frontal photographs. The decision is in the best interests of all parties. Only one item remains to complete my dress apparel. Location of this soldier's non-cling slip, no doubt imminent, is necessary. Dress, low-heeled footwear on, procedures to assist and dress other members of squad ensue.

Red alert! Distress sounds within the ranks. A cry for help is heard. Man down! Not on this soldier's watch! Ring-bearer Chris, is shouting "Conkey," code word for his favorite, dirty, spit-covered, stuffed monkey, carried for comfort, companionship. In defiance of known and unknown enemies, Conkey is under threat of removal from him. Will attempt rescue mission without benefit of slip.

Leaving bedroom sanctuary, this soldier runs to stair landing, scoops up and carries said member of squad, with monkey, back to safety of bedroom. Katherine and Thomas, parents of injured party, indicating serious divisions within the ranks, instigated the unwarranted attack on Chris. A call to restore order and unity is sounded. The bride is on the phone again, demanding our whereabouts' coordinates.

Chris and I refresh on a chocolate bar and barricade ourselves in the bedroom to restart dressing detail. Reluctant to have top of shirt buttoned and to use proper clip-on tie, that detail of dress code is waived for the moment. Subject cadet is missing one shoe and sock; a search of area is required. Two and barely capable of speech, it is certain that Cadet Chris's lost shoe and sock is outside the demilitarized zone (i.e., perimeter of the bedroom). We must retrieve lost items by leaving our safe haven. Our mission is clear.

Dissension within the ranks continues. Thomas and Katherine are in a heated altercation concerning dress wear. The first, cannot button his vest and the second, hates her dress. Various family members, myself included, are mentioned in less than endearing terms. A shout of "I'm not going to this wedding at all" from Katherine is creating a serious morale incident! A bathroom door is slammed, and said parties are continuing to pounce on one another in the mentioned confined area. Grandpapa, attempting an intervention, is yelling at both "rummies" that they are out of line, and the bride is on the phone again. Observation confirms Grandpapa is in his tuxedo jacket, shirt, tie, and socks but does not have trousers or underwear on. Alerted to his dress infraction, Grandpapa speeds from area. Definite slurring of "rummies" and other words gives rise to the suspicion he has imbibed with enthusiasm from the liquor cabinet.

The phone in this soldier's hands, the bride informs me in full siren-level volume, that the photographer is on the premises and assuming position with all appropriate lighting and camera equipment. In addition, the general demands we report our exact proximity to wedding hall. This soldier feels this information fits more appropriately, with the past "don't ask and don't tell" decision in another military area. Therefore, full disclosure will not be appropriate at this time.

Orders to "chop chop" are issued after conversation with bride ends, and parties emerge from various doors to unify. Grandpapa yells, "Walking and talking, move it, move it." Statements, such as "idiot, don't speak to me, ever, I hate you," swirl in the air. This person retains her dignity and decorum, and searches for shoe and sock of calmest cadet, Chris.

Again, the phone sounds. No squad member moves to answer. Thomas finally mans up. General Angelina is in tears at the developing situation. She requires our immediate presence. Roger. Understood. Members of squad accept responsibility for our general's tears and race in unison to gather whatever wedding ornaments and/or clothes necessary to complete their dress uniform and run to assigned vehicle.

With deliberate attention and purpose, all members of squad alight to vehicle. It is agreed, after some shouting, that a quick stop at McDonald's for coffee is required for Grandpapa, to effect sobering. Then, with all haste, we will proceed with determination to destination. Victory or death. Oorah!

Unable to locate non-cling slip will require adjustments, as static cling may cause mother of the bride's outfit to stick to rump area. Katherine has only one pink eyelid; situation to be rectified in powder room. It is not certain in this light if Grandpapa is wearing corduroy trousers with his tuxedo jacket; this situation may require only waist-up photos of said old goat. Son's hair needs grooming. Chris, however, is on board in car seat, with monkey, napping in preparation for main event.

Destination arrival time, accounting for minor time loss in drive-thru at McDonald's, at current speed, contingent upon noninterference from police or other obstructions, is calculated at 0600. Accept and prevail!

All is well on God's green earth, and God bless America. Oorah!

The Funeral

Mind adrift, looking out of Kenny's car window, wondering who would want to bury anyone outside of Kingston, much less a tiny stillborn. Bleached out, colorless, paint peeling, insignificant storefronts, and dilapidated, cheerless homes that have broken sidewalks with weed-infested cracks. Childless yards, not even a stray cat or sleeping dog apparent, it seems all happiness left town long ago. Our purpose is to attend a funeral for an infant who never drew a breath among us.

Mother is sitting in the front seat. Pasty skinned, not well, old for Christ's sake, she is chattering and catching up with Kenny. Begrudgingly, feeling a newfound respect for Kenny, I credit him for his behavior with mother's mile-a-minute talking. A lesser man's ears would have fallen off his head by this time.

Mother does not appreciate my hard work to get a degree and a good position at a prestigious hospital. She maintains contact with friends she made at the project we lived in when destitute. It is like a slap in the face. A senior, safe, clean building, among peers better situated financially and more suitable culturally, is where I placed her, near to me. The project is a place to erase from memory. Inclusion in this funeral stirs memories, feelings best buried. Mother had no right to involve me. I fault myself for letting her cajole me into this.

In the Moment

Pulling into the funeral parlor's parking lot, Mother's face visibly darkens. It is as if a hand slipped a mask of grief over her face. Her neck and arms have the same sad pallor. Instinctively, looking at my own arms, I check to see if it is merely a trick of the lighting, but I detect no such color change in me.

Roberta, grandmother to the deceased baby, is waiting anxiously at the entrance door for our arrival, for some time it appears. Mother's friend is tall, thin as a rake, looks like an alcoholic, but her flushed reddish coloring is due to emphysema. Her incessant smoking causes the disease. A portable oxygen unit belongs in a sling over her body, but no such thing is visible. In all likelihood, the portable oxygen tank is in the trunk of a car, and Mother will not challenge Roberta on this issue either. Cringing, I know that with this group, things are not black and white.

Arm in arm, the two friends uncannily resemble each other. As if sisters, they enter the building. Their gait, hair coloring, and funeral dress are strikingly similar—or is it an age thing? Immediately embracing fellow mourners in the hallway of the dingy funeral parlor, the two women in unison begin offering condolences, shaking hands, kissing the grieving. I follow behind, carrying Mother's handbag with medications and a huge tote bag with everything but the kitchen sink. Roberta coughs steadily, and Mother limps purposefully in beat with her friend's hacking. In this fashion, we proceed to the wake area.

Mother kneels and crosses herself in front of the miniature, closed, white coffin for baby Bess. Roberta puts her hand on Mother's shoulder, shaking her head and rhythmically gasping up air, as Mother continues to pray for Bess.

Still clutching her crucifix, Mother, assisted by her blue-lipped friend, stands and moves to the left side of the baby's coffin, and Roberta stands to the right. The tacky, old-fashioned wallpapered room takes on an unexpected dignity, and the two ordinary-sized vases of daises on either side of the baby's coffin, with a simple tiny heart of white roses on top, convey a more touching gesture than any large wreath or arrangement could.

The soft pink lighting around the coffin cannot hide the wet eyes of the prematurely aged women. Their eyes gleam to the back of the room. The mourners, who were speaking among themselves, cease and form a quiet, comforting procession to say good-bye to Bess. Heavy and solemn, the mostly young mourners follow the example of grief shown by the standing women and the very walls that surround Bess.

Going through the motions at my turn, a glimpse of Mother's correcting, soft eyes unexpectedly causes me to weep for the little one. Not having contact with any of these people in years, aching sorrow for a baby whose face I never saw is not rational. I am stunned. Kleenex, pats, kisses from people I no longer want involvement with, soothe me. Seated and asked if I need water; feeling dizzy, aware someone is fanning me; I am still dumbfounded at my overreaction.

Gaining composure, I realize the vigorous and now unwanted fanning is by an old nemesis of mine, a high school bully, Shannel. Two little ones with dark complexioned faces and noses just like my old enemy are staring in wonderment and suspicion at me. They have accompanied their mother to the funeral. With little fanfare, Shannel and the children divide and sit on either side of me, intimidating me, not to move elsewhere.

Awkward is an oxymoron. Shannel's children have little understanding of funeral protocol, and the young brother and sister are waiting for an opportunity to escalate a poke into a meltdown. The mourning mind frame I had changes into a desperate need-to-escape mode. Sitting on either side of the siblings, neither Shannel nor I speak. The children end the silence by setting off a pushing and shoving contest. Automatically, Shannel initiates correction measures. Flustered is an understatement when I realize the measure to separate and discipline the children is to sit each child on the outside of an adult. Shannel and I are sitting next to each other now.

We are a study in reverse, Shannel and I. She is dark in a way that has little to do with her skin, voluptuous, there is an easy about her, and her dress is inappropriate for a funeral. Shannel has a presence, an attitude you sense from across a room. In contrast, dressed in a proper gray business suit, I have a body that has worked hard to remain trim. My hair is up, and I look sophisticated. My appearance is deliberate, meant to reek of success, yet her confidence is equal to or more than mine. To converse is inevitable, and of course, Shannel begins.

"Expected your mama here, but not you," Shannel launches the unwanted conversation.

"Not my idea," is my rebuttal.

More silence until Shannel's little boy leans forward and sticks his tongue out at his sister, causing her to cry. The two go at each other with a passion, forcing us both to stand to break them up and Mother to rush over and advise us to take them out for a few minutes.

The outside air is fresh, free of death, and I am grateful to be out of the building, though I need to be free of Shannel and my past to enjoy its peace and quiet. The lawn is rather unkempt, I immediately notice.

At my heels, Shannel clips, "Lydia, the shit that went down is long gone. Are you gonna be badass about it forever? You got some share in it ... my making fun of you, fighting, and taking your stuff ... you had your part to play in it." Shannel blurts this out and more and then stops as suddenly as she started. We both spot a small bench to sit on in the neglected backyard, sit down simultaneously without a word, and watch the children run about in circles.

Shannel's expression looks genuine, but I am careful not to lower my guard. Is it her idea of an apology? Dare I ease the tension in my shoulders? I refuse to take blame for her treatment of me; on this, I will not back down.

Shannel is a woman with a life story only soap and pulp readers can appreciate. Her chances of getting as far as she has were slim. I understand this now, but at fourteen, her behavior was incomprehensible. Life was difficult for me for about ten years, but her life from the beginning was one of abuse, abandonment, opportunities lost, and finally a half-brother murdered by gangs; she had little choice but to bury herself in the hicks, as she puts it. Jealousy is a component of our relationship, more on her side though. I acknowledge that I resent Mother's involvement with Shannel, the way she still shows her kindness, as she did in the past. Revisiting and examining the past can bring about what changes? Forgiveness, perhaps? Most people, to my knowledge, however, become more of what they were in the first place. What then is the purpose in dealing with them again, forgiving them repeatedly?

"What happened to the baby? And where is Allison?" I question her all at once to wipe the slate clean of the original subject.

"Allison got blood pressure problems, and she was told to go over to that Crusader Clinic, and you know what a shithole that is. Well, with trying to hold her bus-driving job and looking out for her other kid, she was missing appointments, got bad, and just collapsed on the job. Roberta came over to her place to try to help, but everything turned bad quickly. Rushed to the County Hospital, she and the baby were in trouble. The baby's heartbeat weakened; she didn't make it. Allison was here earlier you know, but she went deadly ash white, like see-through, bleeding again. An ambulance took her minutes before you got here. She begged her mama to stay with the baby. Pitiful, the whole damn mess. It makes no sense. Having no fucking money doesn't help things, you know," Shannel gushed this information in one breath.

On the surface, all this grief sounds preventable. Living on the edge, never making ends meet, the loneliness and futility of it—why have another child? Perhaps that is the point; sometimes a moment of solace, a break from unrelenting hardship makes the need for human touch so essential that you take that risk. A child seems welcome, a blessing. The price paid for taking that chance is the highest, and never would I run that risk.

Shannel looks defeated and tired from the telling of Bess and Allison's story; any comment about birth control would not change the situation or ease the heartbreak. Poverty kills. Dispensable people are not whom I deal with on a regular basis anymore. I doubt if I could ever be part of it willingly again, but the lack of equity is palatable here, and I am filled with an unfathomable sense of guilt for escaping from it. Small talk seems trite and useless; we sit in silence as the children play half-heartedly. Time slips away while we sulk, each of us alone in private thought, yet together on the bench.

The gloom from the funeral parlor permeates the outside air. The children feel it too and lean on their mother. A dank chill crawls around my neck, and Shannel looks shaken as we both rise, aware that Mother and Roberta are standing alone by the coffin, without relief. Wordlessly, we collect the children and feel the funeral parlor sucking us in.

Worn and tired, Mother and Roberta look like sentinels who have stood guard for centuries. Our neglect of duty, we regret. Strangely quiet, as dreary as the adults, the children pile on a small sofa and lean on each other with nary a poke or tongue sticking out, and the little boy begins to doze on his sister's small shoulder. Ashamed, we both assure the standers we will stay with Bess the rest of the time. We keep vigil for about an hour and a half, giving solemn nods to the few visitors that pass.

Closing time at hand, and except for three visitors in the back talking among themselves, no one is present. Kenny is in the group, and Shannel's son favors him I realize. Kenny nods to Shannel, whose face says nothing, as he moves forward and rearranges the children, making them more comfortable on the sofa. I am not privy to parenthood information or other personal knowledge concerning Shannel, but I wager Mother is.

Leaving my post to find Mother and Roberta, a light from a small private room beckons. One burgundy-shaded lamp and two armchairs, a print of a traditional painting of Jesus, and a worn table with water and a box of tissues fill the space. Sitting face to face, the top of their heads touching, Roberta's hand pats Mother's knee while she rubs her friend's shoulder. Tears spill between them. Their cheeks wet, they cry for more than Bess. My heart literally feels squeezed, and the pain causes my eyes to water and makes it difficult to swallow. I gasp for breath. Backing up to leave the room, feeling Shannel at my back, turning, her face shows me that she is swallowing the same wad of sorrow. Nowhere to run, I move to help lift Mother out of her chair and mumble, "Kenny is waiting."

"Kids got to get home, Roberta," Shannel states loudly. Her brisk statement of fact sounds like a huge glass chandelier falling to the floor. The solemn atmosphere shattered, it causes Roberta to wheeze and struggle to rise. Mother looks at me, imagining a solution is imminent from her college-educated daughter, though not one comes to mind.

The funeral director intercepts us on the way out. He is like a silver cat with yellowish, blurry eyes. He purrs his saccharine condolences and appears to rub against Roberta as he reminds her of the burial time and procedures. Nauseous and faint, Mother edges me through the door while holding Roberta's hand.

Outside, Roberta has us pray that Allison will be able to attend the burial. Laboring for each breath, she is helpless and allows Shannel to attach her oxygen. Kenny guzzles a can of beer as he puts the children in the back of Shannel's car and checks the locks on the door. Heading to his car, he motions to Mother and helps her load her paraphernalia.

With stoic perseverance, Shannel makes her way to the driver's side with me close behind. The overhead lighting shows her facial lines, and mine must be visible too. She is exhausted. With trepidation and perplexed at my inexplicable behavior, I hand her my business card with my cell number on the back.

Shannel looks at it and me with curiosity, presses her head back on the head rest, and gives me an amazed, almost warm smile as she remarks, "Well, aren't you a surprise!"

Bozo Hair

The Telephone Conversation

Stella: Hey, Becky! Am I glad you called. Man, you should see what I've done to my hair! It's fricking horrible—Bozo red!

Becky: You're kidding me!

Stella: No joking, man. It's unbelievable. I already called the Clairol emergency number, you know.

Becky: Oh God. What'd they say, Stell?

Stella: Well, they gave me a formula ... told me to mix this with that and buy #35 dye. That's what'll tone it down supposedly, and wouldn't you know it ... the damn Osco near me didn't have #35, so I figured I'd try another brand and put that stuff on—and what'dya think happened?

Becky: Catch your breath, dear. Good Lord, I know where this is going. Stell, honey, them boxes all say something about mixing one shit with another, don't they? How long you been dying your hair, not to know better and mess up like that?

Stella: Yeah, well kiss my pink pa-toot. Bozo hair sucks, but at least Bozo and other clowns can wear it well. I can't even describe the red color I am now ... I'm beyond horrible looking ... Beck, can you hold the laughing? You'll get an attack of hiccups, you know. A little sympathy would help. I'm a total mess, and that's the truth. Cut it out already!

Becky: Sorry sweetie. It *is* funny as hell though. Oh, God ... I'm gotta laugh my butt off at you just a little more ... I can just picture you, Stell!

Stella: Yeah ... well, laugh some more 'cause I called my big girl, and she said, "Mama, take a picture and text me. It can't be all that bad." So, I take the top of my head and send it, and she calls back and says her whole factory floor is laughing their "arses" off. My younger girl, my fancy nurse one, said old people like me shouldn't shop in drugstores by themselves. She's got a real mouth on her, Becky.

Becky: Don't get your panties in a bunch. The kid comes by it natural enough, Stell, so don't go on. Remember when my hair was that strange blue color? You split a gut over it, as I remember ... you thought I made a "Kool-Aid" punk grandma.

Stella: Yes, my dear, your hair was a wonderful Kool-Aid blue, and what a scream! You poor little thing ... and that church social thing you had to go with your sister to ... I didn't exactly give up the sympathy, did I? Oh God ... what goes round comes round. What'dya think? Should I call back Clairol and tell 'em I mixed brands and formulas and didn't follow instructions and let them pee their pants laughing at me, or should I get used to Bozo hair? May I'll never laugh at other people's hair ... I better swear to God!

Becky: One prob at a time, girlfriend, as the kids say ... let me think. You know it sure is quiet here with you not around.

Stella: I miss you buckets too, Becky. Maybe I should just get used to the way people's eyes get all boogley when they see my hair ... I'll be a trendsetter ... I could go natural?

Becky: You gray, my friend? Never! I like the boogley-eyed plan myself. There we have it—a perfect plan B. Get it? B as in boogley eyed. Or, hon, go for C and call Clairol. Get it? C ... Clairol.

Stella: Oh my God, you've gone crazy nuts on me! Becky, I love you ... I'll get working on a Plan C ... maybe. Wish you weren't so far away.

Becky: Love you back, kiddo. I'll always be a phone call away. Talk to you later, when your hair's in order!

Stella: Yeah. Right. Take care. Catch ya later.

Anna

Dear Johnny,
    Walt says I'm not to write ya. Ya're not my old man, ya're gone out of our lives, ya're good as dead where ya're at, and he's right ya know. It don't make sense why's I still write ya.

    Walt's put me on a tight leash since we moved from Dixon. Livin' in Quincy ain't no pleasure with him, for sure. Can't have movie mags at the house; ya know how me and Beth enjoyed 'em. Them be temptations, foolishness, says Walt. Good the girls be grown and on their own, a woman likes a pretty. Sometimes I gets to thinkin' about ya, and that's just how it be.

    Remember that time we was at the groceries, me and Beth was readin' the movie mags in line, and ya noticed she stuffed one up her skirt? Let into her for it, ya did, told her we was respectable, churched, and not's to let ya catch her again at it. We's knows right and wrong, weren't no white trash, and each day's supposed to be a step forward. Told Beth how ya did stuff like that when ya was a kid and landed up doin' time in juvie for it. Then ya bought her two of them mags, just to show ya forgive her. That's how ya was, good. That cashier lady, Flo, the one we always liked, said I had the craziest old man, but in a way ya was sweet. She was right about the crazy, Johnny. Whatever. Ya did yellow barn, and Beth don't ask about ya like she did.

Seth run off again, and Walt says if I fetch him back, he ain't stayin' here. He says the kid's gots his daddy's eyes, it's a waste of time. Walt don't see much point in chasin' after him 'cause he's seventeen now. I don't see's it like that.

That boy sure did miss ya at first. Remember how he used to squat down and watch ya fix cars, and drags that big ole sledgehammer over, gonna move the bricks holdin' up the car ya was under—remember that? Lucky for ya the girls come runnin' and carried him off.

Remember them boots ya favored, and how Seth used to put 'em on and clomp about the trailer, made ya nuts it did? Seth wore 'em for the longest time after ya left. All's the while tils he outgrew 'em. Even then, Seth was hard put to part with yar boots. Ya'd think Seth would've forgotten ya altogether. He wasn't that much outta diapers when the sheriff came the last time for ya. I'm gonna see if Massey won't drive me up to Cortland or over to DeKalb to look for Seth. If he's gone on to trouble in Chicago, I'm scared we lost him, if he does ice up there.

Abby's okay. She's got her a sweetie, and they're talkin' movin' over to Oregon and workin' at a church camp. Real glad she's found God. Nice little town, it'll suit 'em.

Why's I wastin' time writin' and thinkin' about ya? Ya ruined us. And I was never foolin' around with Walt when we was together neither. Ya're mind was off. No reasonin' with ya. Ya saw and thought yarself stuff that was never real. Rev. Bob says that meth makes ya paranoid after a while. I don't know about that stuff. Ya ought to've known better. Why'd ya do it? And, when ya was a fool tweeker and cooked that shit with little Seth alongside, that was the final shot for me. How'd ya do that with the boy there?

Remember that time when's we went up to check out that Corn Fest in DeKalb? We put back some beers and took the kids on the rides. Ya was still good to us then. We had us a good ole time dancin' up with that Howard and the White Boys Band, didn't we? They was fun. Ya said to one of them biker boys near the stage that he looked sissy. Good grief, ya was stupid sometimes. But he was cool, only stared ya down. Then, ya jumped up on the stage with little Seth under yar arm and danced with the band like a big goof. Ya gave the whole crowd a hoot. We was all laughin'. Them fellers in the band was all right too, wasn't they? Helping load up the kids and Auntie Carrie, walker and all, into the truck that night. Remember?

Kids sure did eat good, with little Seth finishin' off two hot dogs just like the girls. What a sloppy mess ya and baby boy made eatin' them free corns! Figured I'd has to hose ya both down when's we got home!

Mama had her a good time, remember? Liked them pretties ya got her for the kitchen, and told ya so. Crazy, but I still's got me that ankle bracelet ya bought me. Another piece of junk I doesn't need is what Walt'll say if he knew. He don't hold with the tattoos me and ya got together neither. Sinful, he says. Man, I gets sick of him. I never known I has so many sins! Back to bitin' my nails, eat them right down to the quick tils my fingers burn.

Why I'm rememberin' and talkin' all this? Time was, ya would've stood in front any one of us if somebody was sayin' somethin' about us. Peoples used to come up to us for help; we wasn't needing to be scared of ya then.

Ya was all right til ya went to Jed's trailer that night after the Corn Fest. That marked the beginnin' of the end, startin' up with "redneck cocaine," ya did. What they calls that shit insults us, Johnny. Ya'd come to no harm with a time or two, ya said. Ya lied to yarself.

Auntie Carrie passed, ya know. The funeral were right touchin'. Rev. Bob did fine by her. Yar Auntie was a good one, always come round when she could. Not much left of yar family, Johnny. Walt don't approve of Auntie or Mama's church or Rev. Bob. He not showed for the funeral—a damn hard man when he decides it.

Made me throw out that red dress I fancied gettin' into one day. I knows it was tight, but maybe if I lost the weight, it wouldn't be that showy, but he made me toss it. Mama ain't comfortable round Walt. Won't stay for much if he's around. We all missed her when she moved way out from us. If Seth's not found, how I stands it alone?

How ya, me, three kids, and Mama lived together in that double trailer blows my mind, and all 'em cars ya was always workin' on out back! Yet it weren't so bad, were it? We has enough, we was tryin' to better ourselves. Ya said I did good practicin' to read, even if it was just movie mags. The kids gone to school, and until the drugs, ya was a bit wild but never mean, Johnny. Ya worked. Yar guns was for huntin' or showin' off.

Ya got crazy, swearin' at Mama, turnin' ugly on me and the kids, fightin' in bars; we never knows ya no more. Poor Mama loved ya to pieces. Said ya wasn't a bad man, just had no common sense. She took yar side manys a time, ya know. After a while, there was no way on God's green earth to live with ya. I'm just repeatin' myself.

Three felony charges and shootin' up that fillin' station and killin' that Williams kid be the last straw. Ya should've knowed the law was gonna come down on ya. Ya're in for life now. That Williams kid weren't cursin' ya, Johnny; he was pleadin' for ya not to shoot him. How could ya sin like that? Ya knows the boy. How long do ya pray to fix that? No use wastin' my breath on ya.

And damn Walt put yar black dog down some time back. The dog wouldn't mind him. Big dummy of a dog would only listen to ya and Seth. Walt started in on me about the movie mags I sneaked into the house, and the dog went at him. I couldn't do a damn thing to save the animal. Walt said he'd kill 'em and he did. Poor animal, up in age, weren't a bad dog, just couldn't get used to Walt. Broke Seth's heart when it happened. See what ya done, leavin' us on our own? I ain't forgivin' ya.

The sheriff found the money ya left under the trailer. What did ya figure?

Couldn't ya think straight or keep yar mouth shut? Yeah right, look who I'm askin'.

I remember ya up in court. Ya was a good-sized man one time. But, there ya was skinny like a ghost, and ya had big sores on yar arms. Ya looked kind of yellow with eyes all wild and dark, sunk in yar face. Couldn't see ya no more, like ya wasn't there.

Tellin' ya all this stuff for what, am I? There's no rhyme or reason to any of my letters. They're in no order. The whole mess I write without thinkin' even. I'm not postin' it.

I feel like I'm in the river's undertow. Can't get my air or can't catch my breath, can't get my footin' to get out. I'm washin' away, Johnny.

I know yar doin' time is the same as dyin' and goin' to hell. No comin' home is there, Johnny? I'm gotta burn this letter, just like I done all the others.

I'm standin' over the stove and writin' extra fast now. Light me each page one at a time, and I dump it in the sink. I'm watchin' the words burn from the very first to the last. Yar letter smells up the kitchen, and my eyes get wet with tears. Odds are I'll never see ya again. Wish I could burn ya out of my head. Left me and the kids for crystal, Johnny. Can't forgive ya. Almost all the words is ash now, goin' down the drain.

Yar memory haunts me. Yar ghost walks on my walls at night. My spine chills at the thought of ya. I'm in prison too, Johnny, on the other side of yar iron bars. I hate ya! But, most times miss ya ... sometimes still love ya.

Anna

Johnny

Anna girl, you're in my dreamin' tonight ... only ways I can talk to ya ... tell ya my nightmares ... let ya know it smells to high heaven in this stinkin' hellhole ... got me bed mites in my cot ... scratching like crazy ... rottin' ... gettin' old ... when I looks in the mirror I gets the willies ... what I wouldn't give for a letter from ya, Anna girl ... all my days are with pervs and murderers ... men filled with the devil's sin ... in shit up to my neck ... I'm a damn kid-killer ... doin' that meth done me in ... burned me all my bridges ... got nothin' ... I'm never goin' home ... no chance for a parole ... I'm just a useless waste of space ... I am sorry ... I'm sorry ... sorry ...

I'm transferrin' over to Ina ... don't expect ya'd care ... it'll be no different ... no family speaks my name, I'm sure ... my heart don't wanna beat, Anna ... it's so heavy with shame ... I know I got nobody ... Seth and the girls be grown ... yet their baby faces I remember ... it tears my heart ... is your mama still with us, Anna? ... no one else's to blame for us bein' apart ... I shots that boy for no good reason ... this time is mine to bear ... mine to pay ...

Anna girl, ya don't be pissed about me callin' ya fat ass and white trash at the courthouse ... ya never was trash ... ya knows I favor fat-bottom women anyway ... can't explain myself ... whys I did what I done ... just fool showing off ... I'm not a man no more, just a number for a name ...

I'd take my last lonesome breath happy this night, Anna girl ... make my peace with Jesus ... go in my pauper's grave willin' ... if I had me just one letter sayin' ya thought of me ... that ya loved me just the smallest bit ... that ya forgave me ... that ya don't lie in bed hatin' me this long, dark night ...

Forgiven

Am I mad or what? It's freezing cold, and the Windy City is that—windy—and here I am getting off a train, transferring to a city bus in the morning rush hour and snow mess to visit Papa, who will make me nuts! Lugging a huge container of beef barley soup, cleaning supplies, and whatnots, because my old man "ain't leaving his house and his neighborhood until they carry him out," doesn't make travelling any easier. A bag-lady with three shopping bags plus handbag, who happened to luck out on a decent overcoat, is what I look like. A full day of aggravation lies ahead.

Sweeping snow off the backstairs upon arrival at the no longer cozy or inviting bungalow, sniffing the air for doggie poop, I check the enclosed back porch area carefully to any accident the ancient dog that Papa in equal parts loves and ignores might have left, before removing my boots and stepping into the kitchen.

Papa leaves his backdoor open. He doesn't like his mid-morning "resting his eyes" time in his La-Z-Boy disturbed. In this tough neighborhood, anyone can walk in and murder the old fart and his lifeless dog. Why won't he barricade the backdoor, so near the always-dark alley, and let me use the front door? This is only one of many sore points between us.

"How many times do you think the city will paint over the gang graffiti," I nag him as I kiss his cheek. "Gangs don't get discouraged, you know. The properties here are worth nothing, Papa. Sell!" The least favorite kid, the mess up, the only one who makes these treks on days other than national holidays, is making herself less loveable.

"The doctor's giving ya crazy pills. Your thinking's all screwed up. I'm sitting on a gold mine in ten years!" Papa shouts with a straight face, judging himself immortal. I've taken to imagining a big X in my head when thinking about and dealing with Papa and other issues in my life. That way I hope to control my mouth and temper, and maybe if I make enough Xs, the problem will go away. Already a big X to the brain about his house. I'm preparing for his next comment; the train and bus ride are the best parts of the visit.

Papa is older and thinner each visit. With alarm, I notice he's buttoned his shirt wrong, and I debate whether I should mention it. He'll fly off the handle, tell me it's not my business, and despite best intentions, it comes out of my mouth wrong. "Start from the bottom and work your way up on that shirt, Papa."

"I'm no kid" is what I get for my trouble. "I'll button my f-ing shirt the way I want to," Papa continues. "You bother me, girlie!"

"Nice choice of words, Papa," I answer back softly.

He turns his back to me, walks to the front room opening buttons and starting from the bottom, working his way up, muttering. Has this become a difficult task for him? Why was I fearful of Papa as a child, in want of his approval, another X for blocking to my brain?

Inspecting, I find the kitchen needs cleaning, and the coffee is too strong—way too much caffeine for a man his age. I dump the tar out, take the soup out of the bag to warm, and busy myself scrubbing the countertop.

Papa warns me to "stop fussing" while he sets the table with soup bowls and cake plates for the rye bread and butter. No drinking glasses. He wipes the spoons on a dishtowel, with his back to me, thinking he's pulling one over on me. I see the spots. I'm going to rewash the whole lot but relent and hold off from moving toward him. My old man is obviously hungry and anticipating the thick, warming soup, though it's not quite eleven in the morning as I turn the greasy stove a notch higher to hurry things along.

Papa thickly butters the bread without asking if I want any and comments that I'm looking bigger. I ladle the hot soup as Papa reminds me to get his Heinekens from under the porch. "You don't fill up the fridge in Chicago's winter weather, girlie. A natural icebox is always under the porch," Papa lets me know in no uncertain terms. Salting and peppering the soup before tasting, he smiles and digs in, holding the too hot soup in his mouth a second before managing to swallow the hot lava. He pops the beer cans with relish, and we drink beer at eleven a.m.

Loud, uninhibited slurping and bread dunking signals that the soup meets with his approval, and I honestly enjoy his enjoyment. Sections of paper towels I hand Papa to wipe his mouth and shirt as he continues inhaling his soup and gulps the near frozen beer. His enthusiasm is catching. I dunk my bread in my soup as he does, guzzle another before-noon beer with him.

Our customary table talk ensues. After mentioning that some of my sketches are hanging in a local gallery, Papa promptly deflates my moment of glory. "They must have had a lot of holes in the wall they needed to cover." He wants to know when he can drive me to the poor house because "you're gonna go broke living in the suburbs, what's with your car, you never managed your money right ..." No amount of explanations satisfies him.

Continuing, Papa, moving whichever hand is not drinking or eating, waves and motions how computers, cell phones, and DVDs cause kids to go nuts and shoot people. Video games and iPods cause autism. He never listens to recorded telephone messages, including the ones from the drugstore or the VA; it's really corporate and governmental spying ... My brain is Xing like crazy!

"Just this morning, I fought with a crazy woman at the bank, and from now on, only the manager will handle my account." Papa is on a roll, and steam is coming out of my ears. He needs a time-out!

The soup and beer are beginning to curdle in my stomach. Announcing I'll do a few chores, I stand, but "Relax, girlie," is a warning from Papa to keep me in the chair. I know he needs to just sound off—he is alone most times—but I have no patience and rise as he holds the bowl to his mouth to drink the last bit down.

Throwing myself into the housecleaning to keep my composure, Papa busies himself rummaging through the china cabinet, shouting, "Jesus, Joseph, and Mary!" He can't find his checkbook, the VA sent a letter, there's a past-due statement, and Papa yammers to me, "Why don't your brother and sister call or come see me?"

"I don't know," I answer shortly. "They don't call me either."

Trying to hold my temper as I scrub the bathroom sink, making a paste of Comet in the tub, Papa stands over me, papers in hand, watching me clean and giving opinions on immigration, parking meters downtown, and why the whole world is going to hell and high water.

"Quit fussing about. You used so much cleaning powder it's going up my nose. You're just like your mama, always trying to fix something," he complains.

I explode. "Don't go there, Papa! Mama was a saint to put up with you. You drove her in the ground, damn you! Your temper and running around." I'm flying now, finishing my rant by threatening to walk out and never come back. His face is crestfallen. Some things shouldn't be said, and I am ashamed at my outburst.

Hurt, Papa lowers his head. "You don't disrespect your Papa; your mother wouldn't have it. And, girlie, never, not ever would I have left your mother; divorce is a sin! I'm used to being on my own, and don't let the door hit you on the way out!" Papa shouts at me.

I feel like a rat, and my temper tantrum has more to do with me than him today. Even if I spoke the truth, nothing's black and white. Papa shuts up and sits with his hand to his mouth, and that's worse than his prattle. I move to go, pick up my coat, hesitate, and turn round.

"Come on, Papa, let's go to the Polish deli on Milwaukee Avenue for some summer sausage and black bread. I'll make some of those sandwiches with the Thousand Island dressing you like before I go, okay?" Papa goes for his coat without speaking. He's pissed, and I won't get off easy this time.

Retrieving his walking cane, Papa puts on an old, faded stocking cap. I watch him struggle with the zipper on his jacket, but I dare not interfere. Neither of us says anything as we get in the car, sparks still flying out of his eyes at me. Hoping to make peace, I tell Papa I'll check if the apple strudel is fresh. He says he wants a couple long johns, to be contrary.

He gives me money for the deli. It's not enough; prices are higher than he remembers. Papa's still mad and waits in the car. I'm angry too, and after shopping, I plop in the car without a word like a kid, throw the groceries in the back, and stare at the snow coming down, with my mind Xing things out.

Bobby, who wants to be my ex after twenty-two years of the marriage, doesn't care what the church says; he's going, no matter what. My heartbeats are sluggish and sad; I'm crying and not paying attention to where Papa is driving.

Papa is going the wrong way I notice after a while. Now that I notice, I tell him of course, but he answers he's going where he wants to go. We're in the old neighborhood, parking near St. Mary's, and Papa tells me, "Get out. We're going to light a candle for your mother." I do what I'm told.

Entering the family's old church, dark and musty, its beauty moves the heart, and my neck and shoulders relax for the first time in a long time, at the peace. Kneeling and crossing, Papa and I light a candle apiece. The flames all move in one direction, probably a draft pulling from the inner sanctuary, but I imagine the holy breath of saints and the Blessed Virgin moving the flames of our prayers to God's ear. I don't want to move; I want to stay in the sweet breath of the church and rest my heart.

Papa moves away, but I'm content where I am, basking in the comfort of God's house, until the peace leaves suddenly. Papa is fighting with someone. I can't believe it! Angie, my rival for my husband, Bobby, is in St. Mary's! Why is she here? Papa is wagging his finger in her face. I rush over. She shoves him hard against the pew, and he slips and falls. I slap her face and pull her hair without thinking. How dare she hit my old man?

The priest, helping Papa up, is furious with all three of us. "God's house is not a tavern for brawling. You all know that," Father admonishes. He preaches further about respect for the church, contrition and reconciliation, enjoins us to pray and share the peace. Father's voice is rising as he continues to speak, and Papa and I kneel instantly and continue to pray as instructed. Angie does the same for a while and then leaves. Father waits in the aisle. Papa and I are afraid to move. Finally, Father returns to the altar, shaking his head. We have pissed off God no less and rightly must beg for forgiveness. The candle flames don't move and seem to not carry our whispered prayers anymore; our guilt is overwhelming. Papa and I exit through a side door.

Helping Papa into the car, he seems limp, worn out by all this. As he starts the car, I blurt out that I'm going to sign the divorce papers for Bobby; I don't know what else to do. "I'm sorry, Papa, so sorry," I tell him.

Pounding the steering wheel hard, Papa says calmly, "You showed restraint in the church, girlie. You only pulled her hair a bit, and that slap wouldn't have hurt a fly. It isn't your fault with Bobby either. I was trying to reason with her, but that Angie don't listen to anybody neither. Told her she was a fornicator and other stuff, and she gives your old man a shove—in church! Father should have been preaching at her, not forcing us to pray with her. You were only trying to defend me. I could scare her a bit—key her car or something?"

"No, for God's sake, Papa, don't do that!" I realize he's trying to help. I pat his shoulder, kiss his cheek, forgive him the whole day, and hope I get forgiven.

"Snow's coming down pretty fast, Papa. Go straight home, finish the soup, one sandwich for tonight, one for lunch tomorrow. I bought some potato salad too, Papa," I say as he speeds me to the train station.

"You coming next week, girlie?"

"You know I will, sure," comes out of my mouth.

"Make me those stuffed peppers in the red gravy?"

"If peppers are on sale, yes. If not, some cabbage rolls. Will that do you, Papa?" He nods yes.

"You need some money for the train, kiddo?"

"No. I'm good."

He bumps onto the curb, and I rush out of the car. "Go straight home, Papa. It's late."

"I will," is Papa's answer. "You're just like your mama, you know. You don't have any meanness in you."

He ups the window, makes an illegal U-turn, and heads out. I pray Papa will have an easy week as I run up the steps on the escalator to hurry to the top.

Waiting on the train platform, I realize I am not making Xs in my head, and the stillness is nice. The platform fills with commuters as the outbound and inbound express trains race past each other in a great roar, moving and stirring all the air on the platform in a huge, supernatural way, and for one moment, a still, tranquil air fills the vacuum, with only a pigeon or two cooing.

The local train pulls in within seconds, and many passengers and I rush to board. I feel so at peace that I wonder if one of God's angels or Mama's soul sped through with the express trains, taking my sins away. I am forgiven.

The Halloween Bash

The bar in the back of the Elks Lodge is decorated in all manner of moving Halloween surprises! A huge witch with red eyes that glow and follow your movements hangs overhead, and its tattered black dress sways back and forth with the draft. A mechanical monster at the back door laughs evilly, and an up-and-down-moving, motorized pirate, like those you find on the front yards of young families, in station by the karaoke equipment, is plugged in and working well. Scary, screaming sounds greet as you enter the women's bathroom, and spiders and bats hang by the mirrors and are in the stalls. Further, tables dressed with red cloths and black netting that hold mounds of plastic spiders, some spooky flickering candles, and a serving tray of green Jell-O squares finish the more-than-perfect Halloween décor, the two finely dressed flappers, with fancy eye masks from the Dollar Store, keenly notice and enjoy.

Patty is in a skimpy pink number trimmed with white fringe on the top and bottom, which tends to bunch up on her rump. She centers her forehead band with the large red feather as she moves her new walker with the three fat pivotal wheels, handy basket, and zippered carrying bag, with purpose. She places her specialty cucumber and cheese with dill sandwiches on the buffet table already filled with a kettle of chili, dishes of cheeses, cupcakes, candy, and chips. Her good friend Sandra is in a bluish-purple flapper costume, which looks a bit more like a saloon girl's dress in old cowboy movies. Her dress is trimmed with huge silver rickrack, and a matching headband with a very large crystal button sewn in the middle is an interesting complement to Patty's costume. A rather daring garter under her kneecap completes Sandra's ensemble, and she happily places her well-liked-at-church-socials spinach and green onion dip, served in a large Hawaiian bread round, next to her friend's dish. Wearing ugly diabetic shoes Patty insisted she wear, annoys her, but she knows it is for the best.

It is already 8:30 p.m., and the two friends in festive homemade costumes are content in each other's company and smiling as they sit and wait with goose bumps for all the excitement of a night out to happen, ready for a Halloween Bash!

A woman bartender dressed as a pirate comes over and asks Patty and Sandra if they would like their free Witch's Brew cocktails now. Both say "Yes" at once. As the bartender leaves for their drinks, Patty hands the tray of Jell-Os to Sandra. "I don't like green Jell-O. You know that," Sandra declines.

"Oh try it, my dear. They are very tangy for some reason," Patty urges.

"My, you're absolutely right," remarks Sandra after tasting one. Both flappers, a bit hungry, manage to finish all the tangy Jell-Os on the tray. Drinking down the Witch's Brew cocktails handed to them, the flappers agree the cocktails oddly complement the Jell-Os, and eat a few more Jell-Os from the empty table next to them. Patiently, they wait for the lodge to fill with other revelers before sampling the goodies from the buffet table. It is only good manners and the proper thing to do, both agreed as they polished off their Witch's Brews.

People come in large groups all at once around nine, to the delight of the flappers. "Oh look," says Sandra. "Someone is dressed as Uncle Fester!" Uncle Fester seems to recognize the flappers and comes over to their table to light his light bulb for them. Fester's friends join him, talking all at once. One man in the group is a nun, of all things. There is a hula girl and a pirate in the group too. They all say hi, and Uncle Fester notices the flappers have finished their Jell-Os. He retrieves a full tray for them. He yells for Witch's Brew for himself and his posse "and the lovely flappers." They cannot refuse the well-mannered Fester and have another cocktail.

Fester asks whose moms they are. Patty and Sandra volunteer to Uncle Fester and posse the names of their children and grandchildren and other relatives. The posse members seem a bit puzzled but are friendly and respectful. The flappers are giddy at all the attention and all the smiles.

More costumed partygoers arrive in bunches, and one young woman has a very tiny swimsuit on, with a sash on one shoulder. Patty feels it her duty to go over and gently reprimand and advise her to be careful not to catch a chest cold in her flimsy outfit; a cold snap is predicted, after all. A platinum-wigged Marilyn Monroe looks lovely, and Sandra sighs in memory as the Jell-Os go down easier and easier for her.

Two police officers cross the room, and the flappers whisper and wonder if they are in costume or not. Sandra and Patty offer them Jell-O, but they decline and say "later" with big smiles. "Isn't everyone delightful?" Patty remarks.

The music is loud, the guests are dancing, and Sandra makes her mind up to have a little dance too, wobbly knees and all. The young people are so encouraging, she observes, as they shout, "Go, Granny, go! Go, Granny, go!" Sandra hops, struts, and twirls with the crowd and the huge mechanical pirate by the karaoke machine. Patty, noticing the nimble dance movements of her dear friend with the air-activated pirate, claps and eggs on her friend to dance more and faster!

Uncle Fester is a superb partner for Patty, it turns out. After helping her up, he spins her round and round and dances a little number with her walker. After, he helps her to her chair to catch her breath.

Sitting but a moment, "Give us a song!" Patty shouts to Sandra, as several of the younger guests laugh and join the chant while helping Patty move her walker, with someone's Witch's Brew in the cup-holding section, over to the karaoke machine, in order for the two friends to sing together. They begin "Hit the Road Jack" loudly, and without the machine, Sandra lifts a half-eaten tray of Jell-O squares from a nearby table and swings it back and forth to the beat, careful not to spill. Her mask is under her chin, but she sings with decided gusto. Everyone joins in, and the second time around, the friends actually finish the song at the same time.

Someone puts "The Twist" on, and both flappers hang onto Patty's walker, swishing ample selves to the enjoyment of all. Repeating "The Twist" several times, the two friends marvel at the talent and enthusiasm of the young. "Why, they are getting better and better at it, don't you think, dear?" Patty remarks, and Sandra nods her yes.

The flappers and the mom question is no longer an issue. The party is in full steam, while Sandra carefully arranges the plastic spiders on all the tables in neat circles. The Halloween revelers continue to receive claps and shouts of encouragement from the flappers, who are content and planted in their chairs.

The pirate bartender, Sandra notices, is blurry, and she informs Patty. The pirate comes over with coffees and sweets. She explains it is on the house, just for them. "Thank you, my dear," says Patty, "we don't usually drink coffee so late at night, but since you're such a generous pirate, we shall!"

The "Last Dance" announcement hurries Sandra to the pirate by the karaoke machine. Unmasking begins. Everyone looks wonderful but fuzzy, both flappers report to each other, though they clap and whoop their approval throughout the costume-judging period. In the excitement, Patty kisses Uncle Fester on the cheek, and he gives her a big hug back. Sandra is kissing the plastic yard pirate and tells him to be careful at sea. She kisses others on the cheek as she makes her way back to Patty.

Prizes for best costumes awarded, the flappers amble up to the front, even though no one mentioned them. The actual prizewinners make room for them, and the flappers wish everyone a happy New Year! Confused, they put back on their masks, and a kind hand or two steadies them back to their table.

The pirate bartender comes again with coffees for the flappers and reports that the Jell-Os are all gone and they have to drink their coffees up like good guests. The flappers do as bid, though Sandra dumps a few of the Jell-Os she stored in her purse in her coffee, prepared for just such an emergency.

The party is officially over, much to the sadness of Patty and Sandra. Standing, Sandra realizes the floor is moving in certain areas and warns Patty it is best for them to stand with their backs to the walls and move sideways. It is not easy to take sideways steps with a walker, but Patty manages. Sandra waves one last time to the pirate, and they move out the door.

Everyone is especially kind and wants to walk them to their car, drive them home even. The Halloween police are back and want to call the flappers' children for them. The flappers cannot remember any numbers for the life of them, and they do not have their regular purses with them. Patty gives some numbers, but Sandra corrects her with other numbers. Finally, the flappers decide to share their phone numbers and make a combination new number. It is easier for everyone, the flappers offer at the same time.

The nice partygoers seem to be talking together about something with the fake police, but the two friends are not able to concentrate on their conversation. What a grand party! Patty sways, as she tries to think. Sandra suddenly is lonesome for her pirate, Patty understands, but the young people discourage Sandra soundly.

That being said, the flappers help each other into the backseat of their car, much to the surprise of Uncle Fester and his posse. Patty announces that her son has taken the steering wheel since he last used the car!

"Children never put things back where they belong!" Sandra slurs her support, giving full sympathy to her friend at the dilemma her son put them in.

Pulling her headband with the large button over her eyes, Sandra says good night to the crowd around the car.

"Don't let the bed bugs bite!" Patty answers back, and both grannies fall asleep just like that.

The bartender pirate puts Patty's walker in the front seat, and their coats are gently draped over them by Uncle Fester. They will be safe in the car for the night, it is thought by Uncle Fester and posse.

"Who do these two old sweeties belong to?" asks the woman who wears the swimsuit costume and is now bundled in a full-length coat.

"Our granny party crashers do not realize this party is for members only," Uncle Fester says, looking worried. "The only party announcement was on the bulletin on the back wall by the private restroom. Maybe one of them wandered there by accident during Bingo last week?" Taking off his bald cap and running his hand through thick black hair, he motions to one of the real police officers, who decides the best solution is to leave the sleeping grandmas in the Elks Lodge parking lot. They will radio the next shift to check on them the rest of the night. Uncle Fester is relieved, as is the swimsuit woman who kisses him on the cheek. All depart for home.

The sun peeks out the next day in its usual manner, and Patty sits straight up in the backseat and instantly begins wiping the steamy windows with her coat sleeve. She is surprised to see Sandra in the backseat and her walker in the front. Many things do not seem clear at this point.

Sandra rouses at that very moment and shouts that she cannot see a thing. Patty helps her get her headband off her eyes. Her blindness is cured. Both women feel queasy and stiff, and Patty wonders how she slept with her eye mask over her mouth.

"Those coffees and sweets must have been off," Sandra ventures.

"Please!" Patty moans. "That green Jell-O you grew so fond of was spiked!"

With difficulty, the flappers return to the front seat, after shoving the walker in the back. Sandra is pleased that Patty's son brought the steering wheel back. Patty reminds Sandra that she is in a muddle. Sandra notices that Patty has put back on her mask. Did her friend wish to remain anonymous? She too, puts her mask on, in case she should be incognito also.

The trip home is slow and quiet. The women are worse for the wear. Many messages from grown children will be on their home phones. Memories galore flood back concerning their Halloween bash.

"Heavens, we can never go there again," cringes Sandra. "I think I molested a pirate!"

"I remember kissing a bald man," Patty groans.

The car fills with quiet again. Both women are trying to arrive at a reasonable explanation as to why they slept in a car together and acted as they did.

Sandra giggles, "Let's hope what happened at the Elks Lodge stays at the Elks Lodge!" Patty sighs but laughs too; she shudders at what those total strangers must think. Two grannies run amok! Playing Bingo there again was out of the question.

By the time they reach their senior apartment complex, the flappers have regained a vivid memory of events and can no longer hold themselves. Tears flowing from laughter, the two disheveled flappers make an awkward dash to their respective apartment bathrooms, lest their bladders give way. They continued to laugh and laugh.

What a hoot the Halloween bash was! They had the best time ever.

Dave, the Bus Driver

I do not understand the phrase, "Misery loves company." When you are miserable, you are not in the mood for company, period. Moreover, if the company is people just as miserable as you are, that is company you are even less in the mood for.

Life is like a slow-rolling earthquake. It comes, may not kill you, but your house is on your head and that part of your life is over—finished. Stupid I am not. The shopping habits of the American public were changing all along. I could feel the waves and warnings and suspected that my personal earthquake was near. Changing my store's stock—more frequent come-ons, lower prices, or other gimmicks—could not stall the quake. Simply, there is no way in hell that individual shopkeepers can compete with the big box stores like Wal-Mart. You cannot put your foot down and stop an earthquake, even out here in the middle of nowhere. I was not immune to this change. The earthquake came on schedule. I lost my store and business; my livelihood crashed and fell directly on my head.

Aftershocks included losing Mary, the wife, the family home, truck, what little was left in the bank, and estrangement from our son, Steve. A general misery clouds my days. My mistress, the nomenclature Mary used when referring to the store, in the end was the preferable love interest, when compared to my present bus-driving career. My new career offers much lower wages, no chance for advancement, regular hours, and much more at-home time. The extra home time really sealed the deal on the marriage. Less income, my sulking at the home front, in debt up to our eyeballs, Mary concluded we'd all be better off if I went away.

Living in and paying rent on what was once my summer fishing cabin is okay actually. I did love the store, though. Opening up brown boxes, shelving new stock, and checking each purchase with a mind to a particular customer was not tedious work. Smelling the eternally perking coffeepot I kept going in the back stockroom, walking the wooden floors, and listening for the steps of a familiar customer was never tiresome. The short lunch breaks at the diner next to the store, I enjoyed. I often received an extra-large slice of peach cobbler on the house. Smelling their meatloaf dinner would whet my appetite. Unfortunately, they had to close too. Out of business, they and I joined the 75 percent of the downtown-area businesses that closed their doors. A tattoo parlor, two resale shops, and a fortune-teller are some of our replacements. Talking with customers came natural to me. They were interesting, and I miss them. Hell, sweeping the walk in front of the store every day was work I enjoyed.

Consumers only passing through caught my fancy as well. Sometimes they might buy a trinket just because they liked the interest I took in them. And why not? I was curious about them, enjoyed the banter, and would have gladly fitted and fussed over them the same as I did for regular patrons.

Sadly, the farmers from the surrounding areas began to fail left and right and stopped coming as frequently. Still, removing the pins, cardboard, and paper out of the packaged shirts was pleasurable to me. Opening flannel shirts and sizing them on the back shoulders of my customers who could still purchase with me, to make sure the fit was suitable, was my job. I would always start to fold a shirt and put pins back in after a fitting with my back turned, so my customer could have a moment of privacy to make a decision about purchasing. I allowed them to feel in a position to change their mind. More often than not, my regulars would say, "Dave, don't trouble yourself. Just pack it up." If I could throw in a pair of socks or a handkerchief, as a courtesy for a larger purchase, I did. My customers remembered the small extras.

If my regulars were widening or thinning, I never questioned them about what size they thought they were; I knew exactly the size they needed. I never pried, but their stories often came as I did my usual fitting on them.

I carried quilting needles for the few grannies who quilted for missions and babies of single moms. Bobbie pins, shower caps, and plastic rain bonnets were at the cash register.

Do the Wal-Marts sell flannel shirts and baby blankets? Yes. And, they are from exotic places like Sri Lanka and Vietnam, no less. Do they know that Max lost his farm and has stomach cancer and that is why he is thinner and needs a smaller size this year? No, of course not. I am a good shopkeeper.

The ex and I continue civilized, "misery loves company" dinners as a family on holidays and special occasions. Steve will not stay much longer, I warn her. In the summers, our son helped at the store out of obligation. Shopkeeper is not a defining label for him like it is—or was—for me. He engaged with the locals reluctantly. He is a young man with other dreams.

"Why does he need a flannel shirt if he has lost his farm?" I see his puzzlement. *Steve, why must my old friend give up his comfortable flannel shirt because a corporation is cleverer than him*, is my unspoken thought. If you can get things cheaper at Wal-Mart, get it there. This is obvious to him, so why not to me. Lowering his eyes, he fears offending me. "Daddy, you're not that old ... maybe a restaurant ..." then stopping in mid-sentence. I could not tell him how I feel.

This town is not Steve's dream. He will go and not look back. The ground is already rolling, Mary, and you have a house you would not share that will be on your head when your quake comes. I do not say this to her of course. The vacant store is not the only place hit by a quake. Our family is in ruins, and I do not believe we can ever rebuild.

Misery loves company! Drive the bus and watch for the regulars, Dave. Are the bumps and potholes on the streets warnings of more quakes coming my way? A bus-driving philosopher. God, I am pure sick of my own company, and I have had it with quakes.

There is Maudy on the corner, on time and looking tired, as usual. She is a good one, she is—a loyal customer of mine right up to the end.

"Hey, good looking! Take your time getting up. No rush."

Maudy

"Aaaah, you're a regular snake charmer is what you is, Dave, and we all loves you for it. Get on now, you and your sweet talking!"

"Maudy, how can you say that about your favorite bus driver? I call it as I see it, Maudy. Now watch your step, young lady," Dave teases as he closes the door and pulls slowly from the curb, looking in the rearview mirror until Maudy is in a seat.

Immediately, noticing another favorite person, Maudy gives a hardy holler. "Hey, Cowboy, long time no see! How's you be? Your car given up the ghost so that you be slumming with Maudy and Dave today?"

"Howdy, Miss Maudy," tipping his hat, "a man's not slumming if he's traveling in company the likes of you and Dave, Miss Maudy. Looks like you've put in a full day. Take a load off and rest yourself." Cowboy sweet-talks in his slow, drawl-heavy way, using his ever-charming lady's-man smile for full effect. Maudy smiles full mouth back at him, in spite of her missing front teeth.

"I sure had me a whopper of a day, Cowboy. That's I did. I'm a right blob of aches and pains, I is. I wanna work in the back like I used to, Cowboy. I gets nervous talking with them college kids."

"You can't do your old job, Maudy; it's too heavy for you." Cowboy lowers his voice and speaks to her in a soft manner. "You will do just fine where you are at. Give it some time. Work is work, and few can do the work they want. Hang in there. We all know what the alternative is," he twangs reassuringly, silken, and respectfully.

"That be the truth, Cowboy. Life can be a kick in the head, but it's all we gots," smiling again, in spite of herself. Maudy turns her head to face the window. She needs to sort out in her mind.

I don't do "just fine," Cowboy. Not today, Maudy runs in her head. *I just lied to you. Fact is I does like working around them college kids, especially that young fellow from Africa, as dark as the black dirt out here. He knows about me now and why it's best I lift them heavy trays till my back breaks than put up signs and slop food to the college kids.*

Letters dance round on book pages for me. I nevers make them into words like everybody else does. I'd stand me the rest of my days holding them dining room trays to be able to read like them kids. When this young feller all the way from the other side of the world talks at me about science and sometimes reads out loud to me, it be so amazing, the ways he includes me. His eyes light up and he be full of ideas and smarts. He gets that from books, but me gets dizzy and see things backward from books.

Mohammad shares the stuff the professors say in class with me while we dish out food to his classmates. He don't seem to know how dumb I be. He'll go on about some computer problem in the lab, like I could even turn a computer on! English class is what gives him trouble, and he says he's glad I talks with him.

Maybe the professors don't like his accent or something, because Mohammad says one of 'em yells at him. I don't knows if talking like me will do him much good with that one. I'm just proud he talks to me; I be used to his sound. Fact is I loves to listen to him. He calls me Auntie. Some of the kids down from Chicago don't like Mohammad talking to an old white woman likes me. I don't be white trash like them thinking. I'm dumb about letters, but I work and work hard. I do look a fright since I had those teeth in front pulled.

Them twins scares me to death. I's coming outs my apartment a couple months back, and them fools just started on me. Shouldn't run from them, but they just be so strange and hateful. When I falls, them teeth gets ruined. The clinic says the nerves be dead, or some such stuff, and I had 'em pulled.

Them fellers from Chicago give Mohammad certain handshakes and pull him aside from me. They figure I don't know nothing. I know when I'm not liked, that's for sure. Mohammad looks worrisome and shies away from me till they go.

Calling me Auntie be peculiar to some because we looks nothing like each other, but Mohammad says they does that where he comes from. And anyways, in my day, we addresses men and women friends of the family as Auntie and Uncle, so it ain't so different to me. He don't have nobody for kin here. Me don't neither. How he talks, I'm used to, likes I said. I gotta laugh. Sometimes I have an extra, and I sneak it in his apron pocket. He say, "Auntie, don't spoil me. I won't eat it unless you eat with me!" The silly, it be my pleasure to treat him. I plain likes the boy. Ruined it, stupid pride, them proverbs warn us.

Today be such a rush, couldn't keep up and puts the menu signs upside down on the counters and front tables. Usually I figures out which way the paper goes in the slot. A bunch of big shots was by at the college, and we be frazzled to put on the dog and have special dinner menus and all.

One of the professors comes over mad, with the menu holder in hand, and wants to know what the joke be. Mohammad looks at me, and I turns to stone.

Mohammad fast changes the signs in the holders the professor waved at us, and moves to fix the rest. The professor puffs up and tells Mohammad not to lets it happen again. Mohammad is embarrassed from the tips of his toes to the top of his head, and it be my fault. I lets him carry the blame. Looking the kid in the face be impossible. I be so ashamed and keeps my distance from him the whole day. After our shift, I not even says good-bye neither. More than forty years his elder, I done let the boy down. Not reading words to save my life is bad, but mostly I hates I be a stinking coward. Mohammad treats *me likes an auntie, and likes a rabid dog that turns on his family, I turns on him.*

Cowboy dear, you don't knows what a shameful day it been. A gray-haired, near to sixty-five-year-old woman who works for minimum or less all her days because she can't make letters stop moving round on a piece of paper is not just ignorant, but lets another carry my fault ... well, it be wrong. I'm sorry as all get out, Mohammad. God, if you talks to Mohammad's god, tell 'em to please forgive me. I hangs my head with shame.

Lord, I be weary with this. I feel so heavy ... Dave calls my stop if I sleep ... my eyes be tired ... I gotta make it right ... Auntie gotta make it right ... I need me some peace.

Tanessa

A racist, left-behind town, a biker haven, a place peppered with oddballs, the poorest of the poor, and the out-and-out crazy, describes the place our family is temporarily planted in. With the last category especially applicable to the Harvey twins, their oneness is frighteningly abnormal. Among Grandmother's fundamentalists faithful, they would judge these men in the grip of satanic possession. Assuming the twins are racist and hold negative opinions about us, African Americans, I dismissed them as examples of low-life, all talk, and no-action good ole boys, until leering catcalls were part of any chance encounter. Annoyed and fearful at first, observing them closer on further attacks, the sexual bravado is an act, fake, a deliberate attempt to hide something. They wish to intimidate, humiliate, to hurt, not to have sex. Of course, I am still afraid. Rumors abound concerning the twins. Dangerous, criminally ill brothers, such as them, invoke old wives' tales of bad-seed children, genetic aberrations, people to avoid at all costs. I act blind, deaf, and dumb at any chance encounter, but that may bring repercussions at some point in the future, I fear.

An anomaly here, two years and counting, I have told no one about myself, and this lack of disclosure, this distance, has introduced me to unexpected lessons and reflections about myself. Educated and privileged, attending college with a mix of people, including white kids, I experienced no overt discrimination yet made few ties outside my clique, my comfort zone. My father was a Black Panther in his youth, turned politician, turned Muslim cleric. His turning or evolving begot family issues, sibling conflicts, the non-knowing of family members, divorces, and hardships, with a stereotypical view of the entire Caucasian race as part of the mix.

A product of father's political turn, "Whitey" was present in our home but not trusted. An asset to father's career and being useful, cute, and smart made me part of the whirls of committee meetings, gala events, adversary confrontations, and the idea that the system needs changing. That was the atmosphere I grew up in, until my junior year in high school, that is, when father made his religious conversion and "turned." Family dynamics changed dramatically, and divorce followed; we joined the ranks of father's first family. Going my own way until marriage, to a man just like my father, a man whose personal life comes first, a man you have to take each "turn" with, without question. A man I ran from.

Will Sees Rebecca for the First Time

Head, go blank! Will it be better when my car's parts come in and I'm back driving? No. What's the fix for a big puncture wound to the heart? Time passes, but my head won't let it be. I pick and pick at the scab; it can never heal.

Ellen Rose was a beautiful child. My frail little daughter only wanted to live, stay with her less than perfect family. Twelve when she passed, small, only beginning to bud, a tiny little whiff of a gal, a slight man like myself could lift her with one arm.

Her stepbrother, a big strapping football player, in high school at the time, handled her carefully; she was a fragile glass doll he loved. After suction treatments, she would cuddle on the boy's neck, and he never pushed her away. I will always love that boy, though he's a grown man now, in Afghanistan, God keep him.

Her mama loved her too but was scared of Ellen Rose, hesitant to touch her. Afraid for the day when her lungs would fill and no amount of suction equipment could make it better. An uncomplaining child, aware she frightened her mama, Ellen Rose saw her mama's drinking get worse, no doubt thought she was at fault.

At the hospital that night, Ellen Rose was so weak, near the end. Her mama could not stay, left for the tavern, got in it with those crazy twins. I'd no choice but to go after her, protect her from those animals. They beat the hell out of me and her, me the most, and I arrived unconscious at the hospital. Ellen Rose died in the arms of Michael, her loving stepbrother, way too much of tragedy for a fifteen-year-old to handle alone. A huge scab covers my heart from the memory of it all. For the longest time there has been no joy in my life.

Those who say that Ellen Rose was better to have never drawn a breath can go to hell. She was sunshine, grace, a tiny hero that stood for life, no matter the slap-downs. Damn their eyes; my daughter was a better human than any, never a burden, a blessing I had for twelve years. I am obligated to live as she did; she was a gift, redemption, an example.

Dave is making another stop. The bus is half-full now. By the end of the line, we'll be standing on one another's toes. Township won't fork over for a larger bus. Sixteen passengers is about the limit of the rickety old ride, but Dave gathers us in somehow.

Man! Someone's pushing a huge suitcase up the bus steps. That's going to take up room. Dave looks like he's getting up, but he's a big man and naturally slow on his feet. The suitcase is going back down the steps. I'm up to check it out.

Will you look at that? A well-rounded rump in a dark blue skirt is backing up the steps, and it's part to a mighty handsome-looking woman. She's rolling her eyes and pulling her luggage up the bus steps. Dave is reacting finally, trying to help, but he takes up room, and she manages without him or me.

I sit back down.

Look at her! She's all fancy in her tight business suit and white shirt. The buttons are all working hard to stay closed. What fine chubby knees she's got! I can't help but notice. Her hair is sticking up on her head. It suits her glued up like that. You can't help but smile; she's swinging a big old purse and digging for bus fare. On her other shoulder is the strap for her laptop case. She's something else, and when she turns sideways, she's still got stuff going for her.

She's like a beautiful turtle. Armored on the outside, she keeps the soft insides safe and warm. My fool mouth is grinning so wide it's like it has been pulled all the way to my damn ears. What is the matter with me? Where was my head two seconds ago?

She is telling Dave she's from out of town, and he's smiling like a fool too. Does this bus go to the River Grove Hotel, she wants to know. Dave says smart like, "Honey, this bus is the only bus in town, and it stops at the only hotel in town."

She rolls her eyes at him and looks him straight in the face and coos, "You're a darling for telling me that!"

Ooooweee, Dave! You better watch your mouth, and don't even think you can talk familiar to her. She's smart, sassy, and not to be taken lightly.

She moves her belongings, heading toward the rear of the bus. Should I help? She asks Maudy politely if she could lean some of her "junk" near her. She explains that her client didn't show, she's overpacked, this and that, and asks Maudy to kindly excuse her. Maudy asks her flat out why she has two purses. The woman explains respectfully that one's a computer case. She puts her hand out and tells Maudy her name is Rebecca. Maudy sits a little taller and enjoys the talk about clients and business and such like. Rebecca only has kindness on her lips for Maudy. It's sweet to watch them.

My turtle is moving again. Tanessa's boy gets a low five and wink as she continues. She nods to her daughter. Rebecca is looking straight at me!

You'd think I'd show some sense and stop acting like I'd never seen a woman before. My eyes are just as brainless as my mouth apparently. I'm beaming at her. Hell!

She rolls her eyes and glares. I'm paralyzed in big smile still. For the life of me, I can't compose myself. She leans in a little to me, and I get a whiff of her. She smells so good, not too sweet and perfumed, just good. I stir like a man.

She stands straight, tilts her head to one side. Moving back one shoulder, she puts her hand on her hip. God, if that ain't a "put up or shut up" look, then I've never seen one. I want to blurt out, "Damn, I'll put up!"

We sit staring and sizing each other up. My face remains one banana-shaped happy smile. Her eyes are rolling in her head. What's to do? I tip my hat.

She blinks and lowers her eyes and gives me the smallest smile. I'm made. If I were a schoolboy, I would mess my drawers with cum. She's remarkable. She makes you catch your breath.

Across from me, she sits, tapping on the computer. I'm smiling, and my scabby heart is racing.

Dave and the Harvey Twins

Cowboy tips his hat as he boards and shakes my hand in his usual manner. He is an understandable man. When I ponder unfathomable things and people, it does not include me and him. Sure, I lost my store, family, and drive a small-town bus for a living—not the best example of what to do with your life. Mistakes are made. I didn't come from a perfect family and saw many things I wish I hadn't. There is order about me though, some explanation as to why I'm the way I am. My life is an easy read compared to some.

The Harvey twins are another matter; there's no sense to be made of them. An environmental mishap, an oil spill, describes them. They are a menace from day one and continue causing disasters as they spread. The Harvey family literally slithered into the area some eight years ago, and on and off has hurt half the people that live here.

I saw the mother when they first came to town, propped up with large couch pillows on either side of her in their car on a very hot day in August. She looked dead from where I was sweeping the walk in front of my store. I hurried to the open window of the car to check on her. Cringing at her bright pink skin, as if she had been scrubbed clean within an inch of her life, she was thin as paper. The undertaker forgot to shut the eyes of a corpse was the impression she gave, and she acknowledged nothing I said. Instinctively, I went to take her pulse. Hand shaking, afraid I might crush her delicate wrist bones, I tried to feel for a heartbeat; she must have a pulse.

In one blink of an eye, two large but not gigantic men rushed at me out of nowhere. They are like an indescribable force of nature. Bob and Bill Harvey may appear normal enough standing apart, but when charging, I swear their bodies combine and alter. A ferocious unit, they became an ancient Goliath, out to murder a David, and me with no slingshot.

The rational part of my mind assumes one of the twins must have grabbed me in a chokehold and threw me to the ground. With me out of air temporarily, the other twin, using leverage, lifted and tossed me. My senses say the twins are one, and though I'm a heavy man, not quick but surely big enough, I'm not easy to just pick up and fling through the air. While making an effort to rise, the Harveys divide and proceed to kick me on both sides with steel-toe footwear and outlandish glee. Maybe they wanted to make sure I was bruised evenly. They snarled and panted in unison as their boots hurt every crack and cranny I own, and I swear they kissed each other and groaned lovingly twice. My eyes are swelling shut but open enough to know what I saw.

I try to plead, explain that I was only checking on their mom, at first. It is obvious, however, you cannot reason with crazy. Fighting back is useless when the twins can be one, and then two again somehow. Unconsciousness followed.

If the beating had not been on the main street of town, I would not have lived to relive it. Threats to my family made it clear I was not to sign a complaint. Witnesses, of course, evaporated.

The devils have some pull with the law. Fights at the bars—tough prostitutes and truckers that roam the highway oasis at night right outside the town literally step aside or run from them. At dog fights, the twins are reported to twist and break the neck of the wounded, losing dog without missing a beat. Some of the toughest gangsters up from the border back down if the twins dispute their cut of the winnings.

The Harvey twins extort the locals with impunity, as they would me if I still had my business. I wonder if the tiny porn shop at the edge of town gets snuff films for them to get off on. Over the years, they've gotten worse, seeing that they can get away with it. They stand out on the sidewalks in broad daylight and intimidate all within earshot. In a sing-songlike voice, with one twin saying half a sentence and the other finishing it, "All you shitheads," meaning us townies, "watch how you're looking at us. We'll cut off your balls and shove them down your throats if you dare look sideways or trespass on our property. We got things planned for the ladies too, if you wander by. Bring them kiddies along too!" The twins leer disgustingly. They'll wink, say they're just funning to a high schooler passing by, "Come on, sweetie, you'd like to try some bad boys, wouldn't you?"

The Harveys are not by any means good ole boys messing and roughhousing country style. They're out of a teen horror movie, I'd say. A disgusting film you can choose not to see, but the twins are not easy to avoid. Don't they have outstanding warrants in other counties? How is it they are never served? Who protects them? They disappear for lengths of time, and just when you think you're rid of them, you're not.

The story is the mother of the twins was sent away to a nursing home and died, perhaps a year or so from when I first saw her in the car. Right, like I believe that. I'm waiting for her wheelchair to get free from the bottom muck and float down the river with her strapped in it.

Could the mother have made her two sons so heinous? For all we know, they put her in that chair. Maybe the bad seed of our county judge or one of the law here is to fault? Was there an incident in the womb that caused the twins to be born minus normal understanding of right and wrong? You can feel they are bonded in other unnatural ways as well. The Harveys are nearing forty; why do they haunt here?

Sounds reasonable that their secret daddy is here, but it's not likely. They favor no one in town. Granted, the town officials are corrupt, but they have the ability to understand what they do is wrong. The officials choose corruption. With the twins, it's difficult to imagine they choose a particular action. It is as if they *are* a whirlwind of evil; doing wrong is as natural as taking a breath for them.

Hard facts like their real names, not just rumors, would help. If they had huge scars or an obvious deformity, you could put them in a pigeon hole and shake off this supernatural aura they have about them. Explanations would make them less fearsome. Do they just plain want to be bad? How can that be? The mind boggles at who they might be, what they do when they are away, what they will do next.

A vendetta is out on the Harveys from the biker gang in the next county; vengeance is required for one of their women. The pack purposefully blocked Main Street, and various more personable bikers got off their bikes and spoke to the merchants while the rest remained in the middle of the way with their cycles running.

They approached me too, and the storekeeper in me made me ask the biker wanting information if he needed a new belt. His answer was positive, and he expected a favor of me at another time. He gave me a phone to keep charged; the only number it called was his. If I sensed the twins were near the county line where their clubhouse was at, I was to call. A threat to me and my family went with the phone.

The Harveys always roll away in time, I wanted to protest to the biker, but I fear a biker vendetta as much as the twins.

This is my other quake, choosing one evil over another. The twins make us cowards; they are an evil that evil continues to dig in. Did my beating from the twins help to put the leaving in my son?

Cowboy sits watching his back, a habit the twins caused. They cost him two months in the hospital. He has his story.

Cowboy and Rebecca

Without the boots and cowboy hat, I can look him straight in the eye, a wiry, craggy-looking sort of man, only the slightest paunch, with muscled arms that have prominent veins. He sports a receding hairline of ash-colored hair with gray taking over the ash. He's a man with a delicate collarbone.

He smiles inscrutably at me. What do I make of those smiles? Late forties, maybe fifty, he's got five or six years on me, for sure. The front room lighting flatters him; his eyes flicker and shine in a summertime firefly-yellow sort of way.

I outweigh him, I bet. Done one-nighters a time or two, but this one doesn't make sense. I'm not down or hammered.

Re-cladding in pressed carpenter jeans, buckling a small-jeweled belt buckle, I watch him tuck in his white everyday undershirt. White crew socks pulled on white, small feet with well-trimmed toenails follow, to stuff in cowboy boots, undoubtedly. Wait. He's putting on brown Hush Puppies. He smiles as he stares back at me, putting me on, no doubt.

"What?" comes out of my mouth.

His crucifix is orthodox. I wrongly assumed him part of a fundamentalist sect because he lives here. Yet why assume that? His drawl is different. I'm catching on that he is not someone you can put in a definite box.

We just finished a long, slow, rather pleasant screw together, and except for that incident the day before, he is a man I know as Will Harrison, and little more. Does he have a middle name? He has Ellen Rose tattooed on his upper left, inside arm. It would be out of line to ask a personal question like "Who is she?" so soon after meeting, I figure. My tattoos reveal nothing, thank God. I'm lazy to get dressed for some reason.

Will asks if I'd like a beer and heads out of the room. There's whiskey and wine, but he can't account for the wine, he informs me and the walls.

We dined before sex, at the best greasy spoon in town. I can testify to the grease. The "best" restaurant has no wine list. I ate a great amount of biscuits and gravy, corn, and chicken-fried steak, plus pan-fried potatoes. Hell, if it doesn't kill the locals, it won't kill me. Will stated he would take me for ice cream and pie shortly. I am being provided a full-service date it seems. It's good I'm leaving soon. I could never exercise off a dinner like that on a regular basis. Hell. I'd be lying if I said the food didn't taste good. I'm not a tiny woman anyway.

Will yells that I can sit myself down anywhere or amble about if I want. I am ambling. He's tidy but not nuts about it. Things are plain, but there is an unusual, blunt-looking nude hanging in the hallway. Is it Ellen Rose?

Fresh flowers grace a small, old-fashioned chrome kitchen table. Nice. Two unmatched chairs are pushed aside a large window. The view is a trailer park and some shrubs. An ornate, colored-glass pull on a worn shade does not look out of place. Surprisingly, it catches the eye.

A half-buried computer surrounded by piles of papers winks at me. The tiny dark room off the kitchen is loaded with stacks of books, open and not opened, almost as if they hold that part of the house up. Does he write? Is he a spy? I can't imagine him as a computer geek. How nosey would it be to check out what's on the computer screen? For Christ's sake, he is part owner and manages a body shop specializing in antique cars. They also customize vehicles and motorcycles. Nothing crazy in that.

I'm nervous because I'm nervous. My nature likes things cut and dry. Everything should fit. I hate it when I act impulsively. I'm from New York City (well, not exactly). Why am I trusting him? For Christ's sake, you have to know where you're at, who you're with. What if he's a crazy?

Why this place is calming and has a serene air about it is beyond me.

Returning to room of origin (i.e., the bedroom) moving freely, my eye catches a very ornately framed copy of a haloed Madonna and Christ Child on his bedroom wall. Missed it during sex. I touch my crucifix instinctively. On my safari, I'm bold-faced looking through, touching, and picking up his things before I realize Will is behind me. He gently puts his head on my shoulder and is breathing on my neck.

"I'm looking at your stuff," I say it like it's a perfectly natural thing to be doing.

He smiles and reaches for his shirt draped on the dresser top. Is he checking me out? I got a nerve, and I know it.

My edgy nature is taking over, and my mind rushes back to its usual uneasy, nontrusting mode. I'm a bold-faced snoop and expect rejection. I fill the air with talk. Talk. Talk. Talk. He puts his hand up to stop me.

"Stay as long as you like, Rebecca. Go through the drawers, check the medicine cabinet, drift through my papers. You know, make yourself at home," he says with a smile and a twinkle.

From his throat, "I'd be happy for the company." I almost sigh aloud. Why is this man a turn-on?

This is nuts. He works at a garage and has a mysterious desk. I work on the twenty-second floor of a corporate branch in New York. I'm here to push crap on Wal-Mart and other chains. So what if we both read and like sex? Lots of people do. Who is Ellen Rose?

It's a painful spot he's had her named tattooed on. My head never stops.

"I've got to rebook my ticket home; my whole schedule is screwed up!"

I escape the bedroom and plop on his sofa, open my laptop, and scan flight-home prices. My bare butt is hanging out of my thong panties, and the leather sofa feels cold. I didn't put back on my skirt before I reambled! Rude of me to park my naked behind on a stranger's sofa. I'm embarrassed and blushing, though I do not want to show it. I try to wiggle over for a cushion. My skirt is in the bedroom. Will just smiles. It's like he can't believe what he is seeing. He is trying not to laugh out loud. And, yes, I would throw a fit if he had had his bare butt on my furniture. He is looking at me in a figuring way. If I must take my head with me, you'd think I'd use it.

"I have on my suit jacket and camisole. I'm half-dressed," I say in a haughty manner in answer to his look, and, "Perhaps I have more expectations from you!" Cowboy flashes a smile a mile wide. My eyes roll.

Trying to concentrate, I see out the corner of my eye that he is busy pretending to put things in boxes and tying up everything with tape and string, making fun at how anal I can be. How annoying! I'm not stupid. I know what he is doing and thinking about me!

There are only two discount flights available, tomorrow at 4:30 a.m. or Tuesday at 6:00 p.m. Ferociously, he keeps on packing invisible boxes. I hit Tuesday.

"You made me enter Tuesday!"

Will is LOL and claims he will soon split a gut. "You're easy, sugar." Tears in his eyes from laughing. "Smoke is coming out your ears. Where do you get the energy to think so much?"

A shove is what he gets from me, and he trips over his boots or his own two feet. I straddle him without even thinking with my hand up ready to—I don't know what on that!

Damn! I scratch my butt on his sparkly belt buckle. It smarts.

"Whoever invented those fancy panties and bikini waxing sure don't like the ladies. Now my fine lady has a scratch on her behind." He looks serious, worried even. "Are you all right, Rebecca? Get off me. Let me see."

"Oh please!" Why did I wear this underwear, and how do I walk nonchalant-like to the bedroom for my skirt?

His eyes soften and seem lusher. I cool off instantly. He is worried about my butt. "I'm the one acting like a fool. Sorry. I didn't mean to knock you to the ground. I ... I ..."

"Can I have a kiss?" He takes off his belt. He and his mouth wait. His lips seem sincere.

"What?" I say hoarsely.

I kiss him sweetly for some reason. I kiss his eyes, his cheeks, and run my tongue around his ears. He catches his breath and smiles like he is buzzed. His fingers get tangled in my gelled hair, but he continues to smile. He moves his neck for me to kiss. I kiss his vulnerable, girly collarbone. Clothes get off.

His dick I suck gently. I stroke his chest, and for some reason, I kiss his Ellen Rose tattoo. We continue in that vein. He gives me oral sex and then smells my armpits, and it tickles and I like it. Each thrust is a little deeper, and between the clitoris thing and the armpit smelling, it all hits the jackpot, and we're both done near the same time. It all feels new and natural, unworked at. Pooped, we lay sticky together.

To break it up, I yell, "Oh, damn, the ice cream parlor. We'll be late! This town will roll up the sidewalks any minute now. Are you trying to cheat me out of my full-service date, mister?"

"No, ma'am! Just pull on your panties and put on your skirt. Or better yet, I got some boxers that'll fit you. You don't need your fanny hanging out big-city like with me. Come on now, tuck and roll. Move it, move it."

We push and shove each other like teenagers. I put on his

boxers, skirt. I haven't time for a bra. The jacket will hide loose tits hopefully.

"Woman, move! It's ten to eight, and they close at eight." We push each other at the door. In the car, Will guns the motor, and we drag down the main street.

The serving girl is a teen with pink plastic earrings, and her boyfriend is waiting for her shift to end. A pint of strawberry and rocky road and an apple pie to go is put in containers in all haste, and we are practically pushed out the door with shrugs and confused snickers from the kids. The store lights go off immediately. I'm sure the kids are kissing and giggling.

"Will, thank you for a wonderful time," I blurt out.

"The pleasure is all mine. I'm glad I get to keep you until Tuesday, Rebecca. You're something else—smart, tough, quirky, kind, and damn sexy when you want to be. I admired you ever since that first time you stepped on that bus. It was hard for you not to roll your eyes at biscuits and gravy. You roll your eyes all the time, you know. It would get on a lesser man's nerves. But, you held yourself well tonight. A true woman, to my mind. I don't think I'd tire of knowing more about you."

"Ditto," I say and mean it.

The Killing

"What the hell are those crazy fucks doing here?" I blurt out loudly, unmindful of the women and children on my bus. As if the random, unpredictable evil the twins create ever needs a reason to appear anywhere.

Blocking the bus turnaround, the twins are in wait, leaning on the side of their pickup. Gripping the steering wheel tightly, heart racing, I slam on the brakes, tossing Maudy to the floor. Tanessa and her two children, along with Cowboy and Rebecca, are slammed forward in the process as well, but do not fall to the bus floor. Maudy yelps, but I have to get out of here fast before I can check on her.

Instinct takes over. If I try a U-turn, the bus will be straddling the road, too much back and forth to straighten it out; we make easy targets for whatever the hell they are up to. Backing up at full speed, my mind races. Getting my passengers out of harm's way is my one goal.

Out-maneuvering me, the twins drive their revved-up pickup with furious speed on the slanting shoulders of the small road, creating a little dustbowl. The bus is circled and blocked again. Braking hard, and this time throwing Cowboy, standing next to me the whole time, full force against the rail by the entry steps. Whether I move forward, back, or turn, the clumsy, ancient equipment I drive is no match for the sleek pickup. The bus stalls.

The turnaround should be eliminated on the route; the trains no longer stop out here. Isolated and overgrown with stink trees and brush, only the occasional freight train flies by. It's a bad section of the county, day or night, and no one stays long here unless looking for trouble. A dump now, refrigerators, burned-out cars, and trash litter the area. Coyotes and wild dogs roam at dusk. A dead end with barely room for a vehicle to turn around in, and now the twins are here. To spawn what chaos? Whose hand rocked the twins' cradle?

Following intuition, I fumble through my toolbox looking for something to use for defense purposes. I collect the cell the bikers gave me that I keep in the box too and put it in my shirt pocket.

Gunning the motor, the stalled bus still won't start. In the side mirror, I see the brothers heading toward us, armed with crowbars and metal bats; hunting rifles are most likely in their pickup. I shudder. The twins, two creatures with firefly-yellow eyes, have the hugest black pupils I've ever seen. Crazed, hyped-up on God-knows-what, the brothers separate and pound on either side of the bus, hollering for me to open the doors.

"Let us in, Davey. We're coming in, Davey boy!" They jump up and lick the windows, chanting, "We want black cunt! Hey New York cunt, Maudy, come out, Maudy, come out Maudy."

Rebecca pounds back on the window, "I got the cops on the phone, assholes!"

They know she's lying and call her bluff, "Come on, New York City, give us the phone. We'll have a chitchat with Sheriff Bobby too." Everyone knows service out here is iffy at best, except Rebecca of course.

The taunting of the women continues; the twins like the scaring part. I can't get the sheriff on my phone either. I warn Tanessa to hide the children under the seat and continue to try to move the bus and contact my dispatcher, to no avail.

In my mirror, I see Maudy is ashen and holding her left arm, in a panic, thinking she could be having a heart attack. I grab my largest wrench, ready to confront the twins, not realizing my seatbelt is still fastened; I'm unable to rise. Featherweight Cowboy, always one step ahead of me, pulls the door switch, and at a run, he wails into the twins.

"Devils!" Cowboy shouts, flaying at one and then the other brother, while I fumble out the door with my wrench held high, head and heart filled with the crying of frightened children, the cussing of Rebecca, and the ominous silence of Maudy. The twins look heinous. Will they kill us all?

Cowboy is a man you want on your side. He puts up a mean fight and goes at them with his all, but in a dancelike move, the brothers lift and toss him. Cowboy lands with a cruel sounding thump. Coiled in a fetal position, both brothers kicking mercilessly, Cowboy is defenseless. With raised wrench swinging at either twin, I try to break up the melee, but the brothers do their magic act, split, and move in an instant. One brother grabs the wrench and hits me so hard in the back with it that my knees buckle. I am just too slow, too confounded by them.

Panting with effort, I get to my feet, charge, and throw my full weight on one brother, breaking his focus on Cowboy. Two feet to the gut is the reply from the other twin. It floors me completely, and I become the new punching bag.

The women are screaming epithets. They have attracted their attention. In unison, the twins move from Cowboy and me and return to banging on the bus, laughing with malice. I try to roll; I don't want them zoning in on the women. I can just make out the determined face of Tanessa in the driver's seat. I hear the engine turn over. Go, go, try to move forward, try to get over the tracks! I want to shout it aloud, but I'm unable to get my air up. The bus does not turn over. The biker phone is still in my pocket. Will it work? I push the button to dial, "Dave, the bus driver, the turnaround." Dead. Did they hear me? I hear nothing. It's hopeless.

Still rolling, nearer the bus I can hear the screams of the children; a crowbar opened the doors, obviously. One twin is banging on equipment to disable the bus radio. I'm crawling on all fours, breathing with effort; things will get worse.

Cowboy rallies. Dazed and staggering, he is dragging my wrench as he passes me to defend the women. Does he realize the women are deadly quiet because each brother holds a child around the neck?

The twins have their back to the front door, allowing Cowboy, in his soft manner, to creep on board and swing the wrench. The height and size difference between the twins and him is significant, plus the beating he has endured makes the blow less effective. It lands on a shoulder of one brother, causing him pain, but not knocking him out. Tanessa's boy is freed from the death grip around his neck, due to Cowboy's action.

The twins are more occupied than expected, enabling me to crawl up the bus stairs. I still can't stand, though, because my gut hurts so badly. I make my effort to stop the twins by taking hold of the legs of the brother still holding the other child, trying to unbalance him or pull him down. I'm a heavy son of a gun, and I'm deliberate; he has to let the kid go to be rid of me, as the other twin is reoccupied with Cowboy. He lets the little girl go, and I'm the target.

Tanessa scoops her children up and pushes them way under the backseat, and the good-sized women join forces and try to pull the brothers off Cowboy and me. Maudy and Tanessa are crying while Rebecca shouts at the twins. Somehow, however, a brother manages to throw a bat at Maudy; her pain we all feel. Her cry alarms us a split second, and the brothers seem to get a second wind. Tanessa rolls Maudy nearer the children and rushes back, throwing things, while Rebecca, the fiercest, hits one brother in the face with her computer, but it only stuns him. I sense our attempts are useless.

The character and drugs make the twins invincible to pain; as a magician's assistant keeps the audience distracted, one brother manages to shift slightly. The other one grabs our poor Maudy and puts a knife to her throat. Piranha in a feeding frenzy describes them; the filthy cowards attack the weakest. We pull back as they know we will. Barely noticed, the other brother slithers away; he will return in an instant with their guns. They hate us. We put up a hell of a fight. All said and done though, not one of us has their blood lust or rage; no one is as broken as the twins. They can't be satisfied until they slaughter us all. Tanessa's forehead is bleeding, and I hate them even more now. The motherfuckers give me no choice.

The twin holding Maudy tips his head to the side the smallest bit. Do his eyes show a glimmer of fear? He is looking at my shirt pocket, the phone. Even a rabid dog knows to run, shoving Maudy in our midst. Without a word, he touches the shoulder of his just returned brother. The other twin is armed with rifles, just as I thought. The simple touch communicates danger and causes the first brother to look to the pickup. They make a death run.

The pickup peels out, and in seconds, it is on the main road, speeding for their lives, but we hear the roar and see the bikers, maybe thirty, some with eyes like the twins, jumping over tracks, seemingly flying through the trees. The bowels of hell opened up to take home the twins. Bikers swarm the pickup; they have all the hurting equipment the twins do, and more. The twins have no hope.

A biker I recognize motions for me to get the hell out. I turn the bus full-circle out of the turnaround. I don't look back. I just drive. My mind's eye prays the twins die fast, and in the arms of each other, to my surprise.

Stiff and blank-faced, the women, children, and Cowboy sit without a word between them. No one uses his or her phone, no one suggests a plan, no one says good-bye as I open and close the door for each passenger at his or her destination. Is it group shock or mutual understanding of the situation? Damned if I know.

Home, I shower and change my clothes. Calling the dispatcher, I make plausible excuses how the bus stalled before the turnaround. My radio equipment failed, I explain. The approximate length of time it took to take each party near his or her home, I calculate for him. The bus will be in the barn early tomorrow, I assure him. The dispatcher seems tired and disinterested in my story. "Yeah ... ok ...

I see ..." was the extent of most of his answers in our conversation. As I hang up, a claim that vandals made dents in the bus while I slept, I rehearse in my head, and hope the company buys it. I don't want to answer to the bikers. I call and ask the wife if it's okay for me to sleep on the sofa in the back room. She says she doesn't care where I sleep.

    The twins are in pieces, never to be seen again. Too fat to lay on my back on the sofa, I sit up and notice Mary has left me a snack, on the table next to it. Obviously retired to her room at the other end of the house, and thankfully, not wanting to talk to me. I hurt and am a tired that can't be explained to anyone, a tired that will never go away. There is no sleep; I see the mad firefly-yellow eyes of the twins blinking across the room. I gulp their puke-filled dying breaths and sob inconsolably.

Rebecca

At the airport, Will, Cowboy to most, touches me lightly on my pulled shoulder. He helps with the luggage and makes a promise to join me in a while, after he takes care of things. Speaking softly in his matter-of-fact drawl makes me feel comfortable. Wearing his cowboy hat, boots, and a fancy belt buckle, he is what he is. An outsider might assume we're an odd couple but have a long-standing, trusting bond. They would never guess it's a relationship barely a week old. With a hand only slightly larger than my own, Will nonchalantly makes a few small circles on my stiff, hurting back. We part as if nothing of importance happened a day and a half ago. Not driving off immediately, Will waits, taillights blinking two-forty, leaning his slight figure on the side of the car. He's in pain too, of course. I want to kiss him good-bye but can't. He is wearing his cowboy hat very low in front to stop prying eyes from seeing his badly swollen, black-and-blue face. Passing through the automatic doors to begin the long, aggravating check-in for the flight home, I turn back. I want to double-check if he's still there. Without waving, I watch him enter his car and pull away.

My airplane seat is a tad small, as tight as the seats on Dave's bus. It reminds me what a disaster of a sales trip, except for Will, this has been. The howling, then whimpers of those crazy twins as the bikers beat them with every metal boot, chain, and pipe they had, tromps in my head. Like Noxzema helps to cool sunburn, I try to concentrate on the canned music coming from the airplane headphones and hope that it will soothe me. Blow after blow, cut after cut, the memory of the final quiet of the twins, and the bikers continuing their frenzy as the bus pulled away, cancels this hope, however.

My butt is spilling over into the next seat, and I squirm, trying to give the guy next to me room. He is smiling and does not seem to mind me so close. It bugs me, and I am aware I rolled my eyes, thanks to Will. I could never lift my sore arm to take a swing at him anyway.

Removing the headphones, the music is useless and can't block out the horror. Those bikers wanted silent witnesses; they let us leave the turnaround when they knew we saw enough. We'd never talk. Cells worked after the turnaround. Everyone had a way to report the incident back in town.

Hell, why should I feel bad? You don't interfere in gangland retribution. Rednecks, bikers, city gangsters, what's the difference? They're a law unto their own. The twins were killed by their own ilk. Surprisingly, not using my brains, I answered the twins back and tried to fight them, which shows it is hard for me to buy into this noninvolvement shit sometimes. Truth is, it's hard for me to hold back in many matters. In the twins' case however, they were mad dogs; it was an inevitable that they would be put down.

This is not cynical New Yorker talk. It's a girl of eight speaking. A product of an unincorporated little town in rural Arkansas, I saw my fill of similar incidents. I learned early that the law could be a biased and iffy proposition. Very "individualistic" people had free reign where I came from, too, just like the twins in their town. In my case, one mother's rejection of an authority figure, along with her decided lack of parenting skills and a drug habit, was judged differently from another who knew how to play ball with the system. Some get away with crimes, others don't. That fact of life ruined and split up what little family I knew. To be a human being takes work, and some won't put in the effort.

Bouncing from foster home to foster home, letting go of times that hurt me to the core, is one of the biggest fights in my life. A small share of the town's individualism must have rubbed off, though. "Wayward" was my middle name; a runaway, with many truancy reports, I mustered a son at fifteen.

My older sister, Evelyn, married and living in New York State, searched for me. It touches me greatly now, her acceptance and love for Larry, my son. She saved us from haunting the place I came from. Never was it heaven for Evelyn or me, however. Her husband at the time was less than thrilled at my entrance into their home and lives. My reputation preceded me. I was a handful, acted out, and was furious Evelyn did not save me sooner. Forgetting to realize, she was trying to track down our younger brother as well.

Coming home one time, after a week's absence, full of attitude, eighteen, ready to confront anyone, I heard baby Larry call Evelyn "Mama" as he snuggled on the shoulder that she had thrown a dishtowel over. Larry was resting his head on a smelly, wet dishtowel for lack of a better place to lay it. Evelyn's kids, my nephews, were running in and out of the kitchen. She had her own brood. My temper flared; I told her Larry wasn't her son. If eyebrows could speak, Evelyn's raised eyebrows said, *what do you expect*? I hated me, but it was my turning point. I was part of the problem, abandoning my son, repeating a pattern of passive abuse, because I was hurting.

I changed. I got my GED, two years of business training, and became a good salesperson. I explained to Will that the business I work in procures the raw material for the manufacture of generic store-brand products. Canned vegetables or fruits, not uniform in size or color, not quite as good as brand names, but a more affordable option for grocery store customers is what I promote. Small towns or big cities, there is a market for these products. I'm not polished, but I can hustle, and I know how to put in an eight-hour or more workday. That's praise coming from the big boss. Will said I was smart but let me know, in his way, that work should not be my only priority.

My past required a smothering, a death, if Larry and I were to have a future. I could not use my childhood as an excuse. I worked to black out bad times. Your past can literally make you crazy, and mad at the world. There is more to the twins' story, I'm sure, but what value is a life like theirs?

Larry calls me Mama now. He is nineteen, a grown man I'm very proud of. He's in the service like Cowboy's stepson. Larry's "Auntie" to Evelyn; it still has the affection and sweet ring of "Mama" in it, however. I contain myself; I slipped at times in my mothering. It is something I will always have to live with, a price I pay for letting the past hold me too long.

Every day, I try to be a little better, go over things in my mind, and search for solutions. Many times, I fail and move backward, unfortunately. Life has to be lived in the moment; the person who just woke up this morning must shine, not the preexisting one. Don't see yourself as damaged goods. Otherwise, you can never hope to be free. Were the twins unthinking dogs? Did they ever try to be better? If not, they got what was coming to them, and I'm already sick of thinking of them.

Outside the airplane window, it's dark, and I can't see what is going on below or what is ahead, but I enjoy the music a little now. I will pick Evelyn up a little gift when we land and try to call Larry. I feel stronger and refuse to let my past hurt me further tonight. I order a drink.

Content with thoughts of that night with Will, ears again covered with headphones, the music blends nicely with my newfound hope, finally. Maybe that one night is another turning point. Hot damn, the man's sweet, sexy, and nuts—a turn-on and a keeper. Life's a mess. I'm a little afraid I'm misreading this, but I yearn to plant a big kiss on Will's mouth, make him catch his breath, laugh with him, and more.

Sandra M. Bringer

Daydreaming and smiling to myself, the thin, young flight attendant returns and seems to sense the nature of my flight of fancy. She hands me my drink with the smallest giggle. I swallow a big gulp and wink a thank-you to her.

Epilogue

Cowboy shows up at my cabin. I'm not surprised. In a matter-of-fact way, he states, "Best we check out the Harvey place before others do." Without answering, slipping on my jacket and pulling on seldom-used work boots, leaving the usual lights on, I turn the TV to my customary channel. Cowboy nods his agreement as I place a box of kitchen matches in the hidden inside pocket of my coat that the ex always sews in for me. Opposites physically, but our stride matches as we head for his car, less than an hour before dusk.

No small talk passes, nor do we speculate who may confess among us. We simply drive within walking distance of our destination, exit the car, and only pause enough for Cowboy to put his gloves back on.

In precision, walking straight up to the Harveys' cabin door, we try to open it, with no luck. Cowboy touches my arm, takes a run at the door, and jumps both feet, to no avail. Padlocked, maybe bolted, the cabin's half windows are small and high; Cowboy cannot reach them, and I could never fit through them. I take a try at the door, using my weight; I repeatedly crash into it with as much speed as I can muster.

My second half moves to the back of the cabin as I continue crashing against the front door. He finds several bricks scattered near the Harveys' half-built grill. One he throws with all his might against a back window, breaking it. Other bricks he collects and stacks to reach the height of the window. Slim and flexible, Cowboy pulls himself up and climbs in unbeknownst to me.

I see light within and hear something turn over. Whenever I do not hear Cowboy, I use my weight against the door. At regular intervals, like a team, we work, and the door quietly gives way. I enter, and Cowboy hands me work gloves. He wears the leather gloves he put on leaving the truck.

A puffy, flowered sofa and matching striped pink armchair furnish the main sitting area, rather old-lady like. Conventional landscape paintings hang on the cabin walls. Some cutesy décor and a bouquet of silk flowers decorate the mantelpiece, though under the skirt of the armchair a rifle is kitty-cornered.

The Harvey twins, a mystery—or are they? They never wore overalls or spit tobacco or line danced at the bar. Many times, they were in khakis and wore expensive sunglasses. Why did we expect a filthy, ramshackle place? Their dressing exactly alike, finishing each other's sentences was maybe only a clever hoax, a joke between them.

Their kitchen is as tiny as in my cabin, but cleaner. The fridge has beers and a box of Cheerios on top. A couple of bottles of hard liquor and cleaning products are under the sink, and a tiny table with a clear plastic covering over a yellow cloth angles to the side of the sink. The silverware in a cabinet drawer is tidy, I notice. Cowboy and I shrug and press on to the small door off the kitchen.

This door is to the pantry and has a lock too, which with effort, we break. Canned goods and other food supplies are stacked neatly on the narrow shelves that line both walls. Some garden tools and supplies are there as well. A narrow pantry, it is only the width of the door, and difficult for a big person like me to walk in anyway but sideways. We discover two handguns, placed strategically behind a large restaurant-size can of soup and tomato sauce.

At the very rear of the pantry, Cowboy and I spot a small cot folded up with a bedpan leaning in front of it. Tucked behind the cot is a foldable wheelchair. Plastic restraints are on the wheelchair and cot. A mutual shudder passes between us. Is this the mother's room?

Moving together to the bathroom, we find an old-fashioned legged tub and wooden toilet that you almost never see today. A large metal washtub and bucket is near the tub, and we both turn the faucets on to see if there is running water for the bathtub. An old floor cabinet has plain towels. Toiletries included razors, deodorants, and aftershaves, all the same brand names. The only thing out of place is a huge, ornately framed, standing mirror at the foot of the tub. For a moment, both Cowboy and I stand in front of the mirror wondering.

Looking for meds and hidden spaces or loose floorboards or explanations, under the sink, we find a brick-size package wrapped in butcher paper. We never think not to flush its contents down the toilet.

Usually these cabins have no more than two bedrooms, and the smaller ones like this only have one large master bedroom. Families can put up multiple cots as needed in the room. This was our last place to look for explanations.

Entering the bedroom, the Harvey boys shock again. The room does not have log walls like the other rooms in the cabin, but painted plaster walls instead. The lighting is soft and inlaid. An orange accent wall behind the bed has a very modern pattern with gold and yellows mixed in. The bed appears oversized, larger than a king, and has a leather-covered headboard. It fills most of the room. The bed's cover is a luxurious tan color with matching pillows using the colors in the accent wall. Two huge modern glass sculptures in reds and golds are at both sides of the headboard and are as tall as Cowboy. The carpet matches the bedspread, and the room is truly beautiful, like a sanctuary. A walk-in closet to one side of the bed and a small dresser on the other, with one foldable chair closed and leaning to the side of the dresser, completes the furnishings, except for the paintings.

On opposite sides of the bed, centered near the middle of the bed, facing each other, were large, surreal-like individual oil paintings of the Harvey twins. Cowboy and I are mesmerized. We turn at the exact same time to study the painting opposite of where we stand, and then back again. Did the paintings capture some difference? Damned if Cowboy and I can tell! The twins appear to be looking at each other—or where?

Obviously, it is the bed, brothers and lovers, keepers of secrets. What I thought I saw long ago was true. Cowboy is ahead of me. He rolls back the covers, and together we remove the large mattress. The bedsprings have openings, and we find two metal boxes with locks, but open. Obviously, frequently opened and looked at.

Photos, many are inside, old and marked up. In the first box, one photo is particularity alarming. The twin Harvey boys are holding the arms of a little girl that looks to be a sister. Her eyes are huge and her mouth noticeably scratched out.

Another photo has a mother with her eyes inked out, and a third has a father with no head, hands, or feet. Other older pictures are the same. Pictures of the twins until at least high-school age are intact, but all other pictures, of what appear to be family members, are ruined. One class picture from grade school has the school name torn off, the teacher's head gone, and all the other students' faces poked out. All the people in the photos, the twins seem to hate. Who hated first, the missing faces or the twins?

The other box's photos are not personal, but the pictures, again, are destroyed in some fashion. Tokens, such as a lock of hair, buttons, a ring, are also here, things with stories known only to the twins. Photos of various people in town, including me and Cowboy, Maudy, and others we know. In one photo, Maudy is holding her mouth and sitting on the ground. It's no secret how Maudy lost those teeth now. The box has Tanessa and her children in it, which Cowboy hands me. She is unaware and in her bedroom when it was taken. Holes are punched in her children's faces. My boy and my ex have no heads, and I have no feet or hands in one picture I find. A further picture of my family at a church picnic confirms my fears were valid for my family. They were always watching. Even Rebecca, new to us all, is disfigured and included in the box. Everyone in the box has pen marks. Is it some sort of Harvey voodoo?

Pictures of dogfights, women in sexual poses and in different states of undress are included. Snapshots of children who belong to whom? Many others unknown to us are part of the collection. Bikers and police doing business, we do recognize. However, what relevant information this all adds up to is impossible for us to imagine. When the twins left town, did they keep another place with the like of what's here?

Cowboy gasps as I pull out a picture of Ellen Rose, taken while Cowboy was sleeping on the edge of her hospital bed. Devil horns are penned in red ballpoint on her head, and snakes are all over her blanket. Ellen Rose died before Cowboy moved here. Did those devil twins know all our stories?

The Harveys are back to the monsters we felt them to be. Without a word between us, we begin tearing up the pictures, as if the people captured in their boxes could be made free now. I continue the tearing as Cowboy disappears and returns with a large kerosene container he is emptying. I strike the match. The Harvey's sanctuary is aflame.

Racing, we set fire to each room. We want nothing to remain.

Possessed and twisted since little boys, perhaps they had no one to love except one another. The women of those bikers lied, I fear. I doubt if the twins made anything more than threats, but who knows. We will never know what the twins are guilty of, or not. Will things make more sense as time passes? No.

Only Cowboy knows I made that call for the bikers. Collectively, the bikers are almost as mad as the twins, their sheer mass in number, so many against two. No animal group can match their savagery. The cries of the Harveys as the bikers cut off their penises and hit them with shovels, pipes, chains, could not be covered by the noise of the bus as I drove full speed away from the scene of the murder. It will trouble my nights.

The silence on the bus that followed as I drove away is an even worse memory. The horror silenced all of us. The devil boarded the bus and rode back to town with us that day.

The Harvey bodies will not be found. The bikers made that certain. Like a scorching blast of fire from a flamethrower, the bikers made an appearance in town and are back in their usual haunts.

Everyone has moved on now. A nephew she helped raise when he was a little boy years back contacted Maudy. He never forgot her kindness and found her somehow on the computer. He wants his old auntie to come live with him and his family. She jumped at the chance.

Tanessa and her kids hooked up with a half-brother out of state. She hugged me when she left; she apparently knew I held feelings and affection for her, but it is impossible to stay here now. A good woman, I am a fool for loving her, too young, refined, from a different world, but I did.

Cowboy has his share in the business and his place up for sale. He has left for New York. He said he'd keep in touch, but nothing so far. I think not, though. His stepson will be in from Afghanistan soon. Maybe things will work out for him and Rebecca. You have to take that leap of faith and then work at it.

Me, I'm back tentatively with the Mrs. It's not good between us, not love, but I know she is grateful and tries to hold her tongue. She has been there with every earthquake. I never speak of the Harvey twins to her. She does not ask. We draw lines and hesitate before we speak. Life must have boundaries and rules, protocols. Some must stand firm like heavy boulders near the bottom of the mountain so that the top of the mountain won't slide into the road. Maybe I can go half with someone, get a business, run a store again. I quit at the bus company. To stay, I have to find something fast.

The Harvey's place sleeps, blackened and destroyed, all alone out there. I never go near it. I fear it and watch for the devil in me.